ANGELA'S KNIGHT
Neighborlee Book 12

Michelle L. Levigne

www.YeOldeDragonBooks.com

Previously released as
Divine Knight, 2012
Revised

Ye Olde Dragon Books
P.O. Box 30802
Middleburg Hts., OH 44130

www.YeOldeDragonBooks.com

2OldeDragons@gmail.com

Welcome to Neighborlee, Ohio.

Where? Somewhere on the North Coast of Ohio, south of Cleveland, right off I-71, north of Medina, in the heart of Cuyahoga County.

What is it? That's a little harder to explain.

Neighborlee is a place you need to experience.

The most important thing you need to understand: Neighborlee is *magic*. Some people say the town is alive. It exists to protect the weird and wonderful (and sometimes a little bit scary) from the cold, practical, material world.

More important, Neighborlee protects the outside world from the weird and wonderful that come to visit … and sometimes come to stay.

First stop: Divine's Emporium, a four-story Victorian house sitting on a hill overlooking the Metroparks. Whatever you really need, you can find at Divine's. Even if you don't know what you're looking for when you walk in the door. The shop is often bigger inside than it is outside. Angela is the proprietor. Please stay on the first floor. You don't want to find out what is hidden and locked safely away upstairs. Like Aslan, Angela is good, but that doesn't mean she's safe. And neither are the secrets and wonders and doorways to other worlds that she protects … and keeps securely locked.

Come in and explore. Meet the people who help Angela guard Neighborlee. Share their adventures of magic and wonder, danger and sacrifice. You never know who or what you'll run into as you walk the streets and listen to the stories of their lives.

Author's Note

The events of *Angela's Knight* overlap events of *Death by Chocolate*, the fourth book in the **All's Fae in Love and Chocolate** novellas, published by Uncial Press, and *Quartet*, the second book in the YA fantasy series, **The Hunt**, published by Writers Exchange.

You don't have to have read the **All's Fae** stories to have an understanding of the Fae "facts of life/rules"-- but it helps!

If you've met P.I. John Stanzer and Dawn Dover in previous Neighborlee books, you have an idea of what's going on with **The Hunt**. If not...don't worry. You'll figure out what's going on in Neighborlee.

Chapter One

Angela dreamed, which was rare.

She knew she dreamed, and that worried her.

A garden surrounded her, overgrown, with faint glimpses of the order that had once reigned there. The moonlight and shadows hid the colors, turning red to black, lavender to silver, and green to heavy, gritty gray.

The familiarity of this place disturbed her, nibbling at her awareness, prickling at the base of her neck. Yet this mid-forest tangle had no hint of the ordered serenity of her garden, not even where it slid down the slope to the Metroparks and gave way to the meadows and woods.

Where was she?

Wrapping her arms around herself, she gave in to the chill that came from the core of her and sent a rustling through flesh and clothes. She wasn't wearing her usual, worn-comfortable blue dress. Angela's fingers lingered over lace and silk and the faceted beads that adorned her clothes. She refused to bow her head to see what she wore. A deep breath revealed the binding of multiple layers of clothes enfolding her.

Perhaps the question should be: *When* was she?

A thicker patch of moonlight ahead hinted at a clearing. Her pace quickened and she wasn't too proud to admit her pulse and breathing had sped up, too. She held out a hand, reaching for the silvery light.

She paused, her hand in the light, one foot raised to step over the boundary from the shadows.

That wasn't a tree on the far side of the moonlit space, but a man.

A man in dark armor, splotchy with hints of silver. For a moment, she thought he was just a statue of a knight, with moss covering the silvery-white stone. Then the helmet moved, just enough to reveal dark blue eyes framed by the slanted oval eye-slits.

Those eyes sparked with fury. Angela froze, hearing the sharp intake of breath. That gauntleted hand clenched and the knight stepped toward her. She braced for the first shout, the accusation, the condemnation.

An alarm clock clattered out in the living room, followed by a slow, syrupy wave of magic sweeping through Divine's Emporium.

Angela sat up slowly, exhaling in relief. She smiled as she

envisioned Maurice being swept downstairs to the furniture room where his normal-size clothes waited. It was midnight of the day of spring equinox. Today, Maurice was his normal size, magic-less, wingless, free to roam their little town of Neighborlee and spend the day with his sweetheart, Holly Sullivan. Less than nine months remained of Maurice's exile to the Human world, in shrunken form, with shrunken magic, and gaudy, glittery, humiliating wings attached to his back.

Downstairs, she heard the sounds of Maurice jumping around, flexing and limbering up and enjoying being six feet tall instead of five inches. Angela sighed and swung her legs over the side of her bed. Maurice had told her she didn't have to get up and make breakfast at midnight, but she wanted to. Holly would be here soon, and she wanted to give the sweethearts a send-off, with a little magic thrown into their food to give them energy and alertness to enjoy every minute of the twenty-four hours they would have together.

After all the guardians had endured in the last few weeks, repelling another attempt to break through the defensive magic surrounding Neighborlee, every bit of joy and celebration of life and love was precious. Kerri and her minions had retreated to lick their wounds. As Lanie had said, hopefully the rock they now hid under was heavy and hard to move. The threat of their return was no reason to hide and miss out on life. Living in fear meant the enemy was winning, and Angela refused to allow that to happen.

Her knees trembled and folded as she slid out of bed, and she shivered as she clutched at her mattress to stay upright. She pressed a hand to her cheek and flinched when she found her face damp with sweat. Her hand shook faintly. Her heart raced and she suddenly felt breathless, as if she had run all the way from one side of Neighborlee to the other.

What had happened?

The protective net enfolding Divine's Emporium flickered as Holly activated her passkey talisman to open the front door.

"Overly sensitive," Angela muttered. She took a deep breath, silently scolded her body to behave, and got up.

Running footsteps and sudden silence downstairs told her more clearly than a closed-circuit television that Maurice and Holly had run into each other's arms and were trying to make up in five minutes for the kisses they couldn't share outside of their dreams since Christmas. Angela calculated she had a good twenty minutes to get breakfast on the table. She snapped her fingers and awakened the few rarely used helper spells in her kitchen. What was the good of having magic at her fingertips if she didn't use it once in a while? It would get rusty and deteriorate from lack of exercise, just like anything and anyone else. By the time she had dressed, brushed her hair and washed her face, the aroma of fresh coffee and waffles drifted out to meet her.

Crossing her living room, her glance fell on the sketchbook she had been doodling in while Maurice read to her last night.

The overgrown garden, trapped in moonlight and shadow. The knight, caught between life and stone. Both were trapped within the meaningless lines. No one would see them but her.

No one *could* see them but her.

"It's been years," Angela murmured, and tore her gaze free by force of will. She wrapped her arms around herself once, tightly, and moved on. There were some things she preferred to do herself in her kitchen, rather than leave it to magic.

She hadn't dreamed of the knight and the garden in so long, she couldn't remember how long it had been.

Why had that dream returned *now*?

And why did he look angry with her, rather than sad?

"Hey, Angela?" Maurice nudged the apartment door open and peered in, only showing his face.

"What do the two of you have planned for today?" She stepped out of the kitchen with the coffee pot in one hand and a bowl of mixed berries in the other.

"You okay? Something felt kind of hinky, just before the inflation spell hit."

"I'm fine."

"Nothing that staying in bed in the middle of the night couldn't cure." Holly pushed the door open and gave Maurice a nudge over the threshold. "You really don't have to cook for us. Not that we don't appreciate it. Usually we're so busy running around, we forget to eat."

"I like sending you off. Like a good mother on the first day of school."

"Yeah, and it's not like I'm not still learning lessons." Maurice deftly stepped around Angela, blocking her from going back to the kitchen. "Sit. Let me."

"Thanks for training him so well for me," Holly said in a stage whisper.

"I heard that," he called from the kitchen, drawing out his words in a singsong tone.

"You were supposed to."

They were all laughing softly when Maurice came back with a deep casserole of waffles and put it in the middle of the table. He went back for the bowl of clotted cream, and when he returned, his smile had faded.

"Something happened, didn't it?" he asked, sliding into the third chair. He rubbed his fingers together on one hand, indicating he felt a residue tingle of magic in the air.

Angela believed when Maurice was deprived of his magic, he was triply sensitive to the currents, the vibrations of it at work, as well as the echoes after a particularly strong or strange spell had worked itself out. She was grateful that he wouldn't let the matter drop when she ignored his question the first time he asked if she was okay. Sometimes, especially after the dream she had just had, she felt as alone as if she had lived in the midnight garden of her dreams for a thousand years.

"I had an odd dream. That, combined with the transformation spell... Well, maybe they clashed. And equinox is always an uneasy time. Especially in the spring, when winter still struggles to keep the land and plants half-asleep. Forget about Samhain and the walls between the worlds growing thin." She shook her head and offered a smile to the other two. "Between the increased Fae traffic through Neighborlee lately, and that whole ugly business less than a month ago with the doppelgangers and the rebel Fae magic, it's no wonder that things are unsettled."

"You're sure?" He glanced at Holly and reached for her hand, resting on the table between them. "What if Big Ugly is starting to wake up again? We're hitting the islands today, but if you need some backup... You don't mind, do you, sweetheart?"

"Honestly, it's not like I haven't been fending off monsters and boogiemen and malevolent inter-dimensional intruders for the past century—by myself, I might add." Angela laughed, despite the clutching feeling around her heart that threatened to have her eyes gushing in another moment. Especially when Holly didn't hesitate to nod and murmur agreement with Maurice's offer. "The two of you are going to the lake and ride the ferry and you're going to get sunburned and have a wonderful time. Go play mini-golf and tour the winery and eat extra-thick onion rings at that incredible burger place just off the docks. That's an order." She narrowed her eyes at them, stuck out her bottom lip and glared, looking back and forth between them until first Holly, then Maurice grinned and laughed and gave in.

She came close to tears when Holly suggested later, halfway through their waffles, that maybe Angela should close up the shop and come with them to bum around the Lake Erie islands. How long had it been since she had had a day off, anyway?

"Excuse me, but I'm a little too old to think it's fun to race the sunrise to the lake." Angela put on a prim face, which earned laughter from Holly but a skeptical look from Maurice. "I plan on going back to bed once you two finally get out of here, and then getting up at a civilized hour."

"You know, there's such a thing as being too civilized," he said under his breath and looked up at the ceiling.

"That kind of thinking got you exiled from the Fae realms," Holly said.

"Are you complaining?" He waggled his eyebrows like a melodrama villain.

She just grinned and shook her head.

Angela held onto her trademark superior smirk, while inside something ached and wet heat pressed at the backs of her eyes. She was sure that once, very long ago, she had teased and laughed with someone just as precious to her as Maurice was to Holly. Not with those exact words, but the same attitude, the same loving taunting. The hungry, lonely pain took her breath away just long enough to threaten her shell of serenity.

She walked Maurice and Holly downstairs and stood at the door, watching as they got into Holly's car and drove away. Whispers, just on the verge of real words, pressed at her awareness. A soft breeze tugged at the hem and sleeves of her dress. She fancied for a moment that someone--or something--tried to nudge her out of the doorway. Outside. Angela took a step backward, planting herself more securely inside the shop. Shivering, she glanced over her shoulder, looking for something moving in the familiar darkness, ready to pounce and shove her out of the sanctuary of Divine's Emporium.

Wordless certainty, a taproot of knowledge deep inside that had guided her through the many decades of her guardianship, urged her not to let anything or anyone push her outside the walls. Not before the sunrise.

Humming softly, Angela called all the winkies to her. Not just the regular residents of Divine's, but all the winkies living within the boundaries of Neighborlee and the Metroparks. Anywhere that magic whispered through the air and ground and water, winkies watched and listened.

She walked around the shop in the comforting, warm, familiar darkness, trailing the sparkly bits of awareness and magic at every doorway and window, every slit in reality, every portal between dimensions. In theory, nothing could get into Divine's Emporium without her awareness or her permission. However, Diane and Troy had proven last year that the most carefully woven safeguards could be penetrated if the enemy had enough knowledge, skill, motivation, and patience.

Then she went to bed.

The dream didn't return. Not even a hint of the dark knight or the moonlit garden. When she woke, Angela couldn't decide if she was disappointed or relieved. Once she opened the shop for business, she didn't have time to think about it.

Until Athena Longfellow called to say that Sherwood, the AI copied from Doni Longfellow's boyfriend, Cosmo, had detected some ripples in Neighborlee's energy shield. He and London had been triply vigilant since the attacks from Kerri and the rebel Fae. They used up a large portion of their energy and attention monitoring and reinforcing the shield to prevent another enemy infiltration with disastrous results.

Last night, Sherwood had detected molecule-fine darts of energy hitting the shield, so delicate and low-powered and short-lived, he couldn't be sure of their origins or if they had penetrated. And if they had, he had no way to know where they had been aimed. These darts were just different enough from the ones employed in the final battle just a few weeks ago, he couldn't be sure the rebel Fae were to blame. Since Angela and Divine's

Emporium were the prime target of the attacks, Sherwood wanted Angela to know, to be on the alert. Just in case.

"You're not going to remind me how behind-the-times I am, are you?" Angela said, when Athena finished relaying the message Sherwood had given her.

"Would it do me any good?" She sighed. "If we bought you a smart phone, so you could get real-time messages from London and Sherwood, and even talk to them, would you use it?"

"I'm … not sure." She shivered a little. Just a few months ago, she would have responded with a definite "no," reminded Athena that she had a very up-to-date computer, to communicate with the AI's, if she wanted, and laughed.

The last few months had impressed on all of them how important modern communication was for the safety of the guardians of Neighborlee.

"Okay, that's some progress." Athena didn't add what Angela knew they were both thinking: the progress in getting her to use modern technology had come at a painful price.

Angela thanked the young woman and asked her how the search for a wedding dress that suited her was coming along. They chatted and laughed together, and Athena made Angela promise she would come with her and her grandmother and mother, Charlotte and Portia, to a bridal fair at the IX-Center next weekend.

Feeling in better spirits, Angela put away her worries and uneasy feelings from that morning. It was just a dream, not a portent of disaster. She had dreamed of the dark knight before, and she would dream of him again, and no matter how many times she dreamed he would never step out of her dreams. She was safe.

Oddly, she couldn't decide if that thought was comforting, or depressing.

The students from Willis-Brooks College who didn't go home for spring break descended en mass in the afternoon, in search of candy and old movies and used books. Angela let the bustle and laughing voices divert her. She watched them, reading their spirits, seeing who had grown a little more sensitive to the magic pervading the entire town, and who had let their ideas of success and their goals for the future make them a little less aware than the last time they had visited her.

Despite being so late into the school calendar, there was always a handful of students who hadn't come out to visit Divine's yet, and their amazed, confused, fascinated reactions amused her. The ones who shriveled up a little inside themselves as they walked through the shop and sensed the magic waiting to burst out, the thin spots where otherness tried to come through--those particular students made her want to cry a little more than usual, when she saw someone resist the call of magic. If they would listen and open their eyes and other senses to the wonder around them, the potential for magic in their lives, they could embark on amazing, fulfilling lives.

But there were always a few who sensed the silent song of magic and resisted, closing their ears and souls to it, choosing to fear whatever they couldn't instantly understand. They wouldn't come back to Divine's again this school year, and they likely would transfer to another college next year. Saying no in their spirits to Divine's Emporium changed them in some way, so that living within the boundaries of Neighborlee became like itching powder in their clothes, or a mosquito hum by their ears. They would flee the irritation. Witnessing this pivotal moment in those strangers' lives and knowing how they would choose always broke Angela's heart. Yet today, for some reason, it hurt more than ever.

As if she had witnessed someone precious to her making the same bad choice, repeatedly. Destiny broke the rules to offer the chance and choice, again and again through the centuries, and yet he--she was sure the person was a *he*--kept saying no, growing colder and more calloused and deaf as the years ground on.

Angela's thoughts and her heart skittered away from that knowledge. She threw herself into laughing and teasing with her friends among the students, pointed out new treasures she had brought into the shop, and listened to her regular customers talk about plans for the rest of their break, or term papers they were working on.

She almost forgot about her dreams by the time she closed up the shop and went upstairs to make dinner. The warmth of the spring day had collected in her apartment. After opening the windows and turning on the ceiling fans, she decided the heat wouldn't dissipate fast enough to suit her. She made a salad and a fresh batch of iced tea and went out into her garden to enjoy the soft breezes coming up the slope from the Metroparks.

"Where are you?" she whispered, startling herself.

Where had that thought come from? Who had she been talking to?

The aching feeling inside her hinted at memories she had put away and even misplaced, for the sake of self-preservation. Taking a deep breath to brace herself, Angela moved backward in her memories, investigating last night's disturbing dream. Perhaps the answer was there? She tried to see the knight's features inside the shadows of his helmet, tried to make out the colors of the garden, anything that would give her a stronger clue to where and when, if this was nothing but a dream, or a valid memory. And if a memory, why had she put it so far away in her mind she had forgotten it?

More important: Why was it coming back to her now? What magic was at work, sifting through the images filling her memories from her very long, full life, attempting communication in those pictures? Friendly magic, warning her? Or inimical magic, attempting to paralyze her with fear, or distract her from something she needed to sense so she could protect against it?

A queasy ripple in the net protecting the shop yanked Angela out of her thoughts. Her heart leaped as she looked around. The shadows of sunset had grown long, like cold, dark hands reaching to enfold her. Her hands and knees shook faintly as she gathered up her dishes and went back into the shop. That shiver of fear bothered her more than the sudden certainty that something was out there, hiding in the coming darkness, watching her.

Worse was the realization that she had lost all sense of time and location, just long enough to be terrified. Ridiculous. She had done it to herself. Hadn't she?

"Enough," she scolded herself, and settled in the main room of the shop to calm down and regain...

She had actually *lost* her ever-present awareness of the magic woven through the shop, hadn't she?

That resolved her. No matter how it irritated her, like a rough edge on a tooth, she would ignore the dream of the knight from now on. She couldn't afford to be so distracted, to let go of her hold on the many threads of magic that fed in from all over the town, the county, the state, some even from the other side of the world, as well as the many dimensions that found their nexus point within the walls of Divine's Emporium. If she had chosen not to think about him, then obviously it was for a good, logical reason. This momentary lapse of hers was proof of that.

Angela stepped over to the Wishing Ball and stared into the dark, swirling, metallic rainbows covering its surface. She could almost laugh at how she hesitated to touch that tool and regain her inner balance and the link with the shop. The important thing was to figure out *what* was happening, exactly. Then she could figure out *why*. Did the weakness come from within her, something awakening, or as Maurice had so eloquently put it, was the attack coming from outside? An old enemy, temporarily defeated again? Was it Big Ugly, the dimensional invader that had tried to come up from underneath the town before? A new invader? Had the energy Sherwood sensed last night come from Kerri and her minions, returning to scratch at the shield around Neighborlee?

Worse: could the enemies of Neighborlee be joining forces?

Closing her eyes, Angela cupped both hands and rested them on the upper curve of the Wishing Ball. She sent her awareness into the foundation, down through the three levels of the cellar that no one knew about. Except perhaps Maurice. She was pretty sure he didn't know the shop itself had dug those two levels below the original cellar.

Then she searched all the slits in the walls of the shop, checking each dimensional doorway, assessing the condition of each extra room that appeared as there was need, inventorying each storage niche that let her stash items against future need or quickly put dangerous elements out of reach of the innocent. One by one, she examined each room, brushing mental fingers over the contents, taking the opportunity to *flick* magical debris into the collection bags, where it could grow and strengthen to the point it would react to wishes and the pure belief and dreams of children. Or those of every age who believed in magic.

Angela sensed the open door in the attic before her eyes flicked open and she looked into the Wishing Ball and saw the two shadowy forms walking where they had no right to be.

"Distraction," she muttered, and dashed for the stairs. A swirl of winkies gathered around her and lifted her up four stairs for every step she took.

Why were the invaders in that particular attic, with the paintings? If enemies were to try to steal from Divine's Emporium, she would expect them to go for the libraries, then the storage rooms with all the slumbering magical items, and then the room that held all the solidified spells.

Whoever had broken into the shop while her awareness was elsewhere either did this hit-or-miss, or they operated on partial knowledge. Or worse, they were dilettantes, playing with their untrained, undisciplined, perhaps newly discovered powers, seeing what they could do, with no goals in sight. No concept of the ripple effect from performing magic, no matter how large or small. And worse, no idea that the power they used had to come from somewhere, be paid for by someone, and then dissipate to somewhere else, with someone responsible for the cleanup of the aftereffects. If they had even an inkling, chances were good they didn't care. That made them more dangerous than the worst enemies who had ever tried to infiltrate, steal from, or overpower Divine's Emporium.

"It's no use," she said, pitching her voice to carry ahead of her. With a thought, she gathered the winkies around her hands. She wouldn't attack--she had no need to attack. Sometimes the best offense was a good defense. "Whatever you're looking for, you won't be able to leave once you find it."

"Didn't find nothing." The sullen, rasping voice came from the darkness of the attic.

A ripple of amber-tinted light momentarily broke the blackness. Angela flinched. She thought she saw an outline of an arm. What was the invader doing in there, to make the paintings restless?

"Come out before I have to call the police."

"Ain't no cops gonna believe what's going on in here," a second voice responded, just as sullen, but about an octave higher.

"You're not from around here, are you?" Angela thought of Gordon Priebe, one member of the Neighborlee police who wasn't freaked out by the strange and unearthly.

Not just because he was a member of Lanie Zephyr's *Star Trek* club, but because he had been part of protecting the town when the weird and sometimes ugly tried to invade or warp the magic of Neighborlee for its own use. If she called Gordon for help, he would keep it secret from his superiors and come up with a good cover story that the guilty parties wouldn't be able to break.

Something scraped, wood on wood. Then something else

creaked in the shadows of the attic. Angela shivered, imagining those foolish invaders trying to take a painting down from the wall where it had been securely fastened with nails and magic to tame it. Or lifting a painting from a pile where the layering of the paintings kept them in control, battling each other instead of spilling their malevolence or unrestrained magical influence into the world. Or worst of all, they were right now prying open a crate, to reveal a painting to the touch of light. It didn't matter if it was the light of day, a light bulb in the ceiling, or a flashlight, any touch of light would provide enough energy to generate a reaction someone wouldn't like.

If she could have, Angela would have destroyed every painting in her attic. Most could only be destroyed by an expenditure of power that would drain her, and perhaps Divine's as well. And then where would the world be? She thought the explosion of ghosts from the detention grid in the first *Ghostbusters* movie was a pale echo of what could happen, as dozens of dimensions and doorways and realities collided in the frail wood and stone and glass shell of her shop.

A louder thud yanked her from her thoughts, along with definitely pained yelps from two throats. She silently scolded herself for being distracted yet again. What was wrong with her?

"Hey, something fell over on me." The first voice. "Help?"

Angela silently commanded the winkies to go into the attic ahead of her. At the very least, they could provide light.

She followed the winkies, braced to duck and dodge if the intruders tried to throw something at her or grab hold of her. The winkies coated the sloping sides of the roof and a soft, pale blue and gold light grew, dispelling the shadows more with every step she took. To her momentary amusement, several crates holding the less fussy, temperamental paintings had indeed fallen over, trapping those forms dressed all in black, with black ski masks. They had to be sweaty in those getups.

The winkies flared, their light shifting to red. In warning.

Angela turned, reacting to the flicker of movement behind her. Too late, she sensed a third intruder. Something hissed even as she caught sight of a black arm emerging from the shadows. Silver spray filled the air, and then fire coated her face. She staggered, holding her breath, enfolded in a swarm of winkies that wiped away the pepper spray before it could blind her.

Hands grabbed her, yanked her around, toppling her off balance. Her knees hit a low crate and sent her spinning sideways. She grabbed hold, one-handed, to a flat wooden bar as her face hit something that evaporated like cotton candy in a rainstorm.

Angela kept falling, twisting sideways, turning as she grappled at the wooden bar. Her hip slid over the same thin surface she held onto, then her backside. Her other flailing hand caught the wood and she jerked as her momentum kept her turning and falling. Her arm muscles screamed as her legs swung out over nothingness, but instinct kept her holding onto the bar.

Not a bar, but the frame of a painting.

The question was *which* painting she had fallen through, which alien or magical landscape she now hung over.

There were some stored in this attic in which no Human could survive for more than a few minutes. Just because Angela wasn't quite Human anymore didn't mean she had any kind of advantage. As long as she held onto the frame, she was in both worlds. Depending on which world sat below her dangling feet, that could be a weakness, not an advantage.

Fire settled into the sockets of her shoulders. She had strained something. Her hands felt slick, and she suspected she had cut her palms on the edge of the painting. Common sense said to hold still, that she would only increase whatever damage had been done to her arms if she tried to maneuver around and climb back over the painting frame. Quite frankly, she had never been the athletic type, and she doubted her ability to swing her legs up even if she hadn't been hurt. Better to wait.

And pray that there was nothing unfriendly down below her in the painting, waiting for someone to drop in for a snack.

Or worse... Something waiting for the door to be held open, so to speak, synching the timeframes between Earth and whatever magical dimension this was, so it could escape. Her hands holding onto the frame, piercing the barrier that merely looked like canvas and paint, kept that doorway open. Even if she couldn't swing herself back up and through to her attic, that didn't mean something else couldn't find purchase in her clothes and use her as a ladder to get up and out.

"Please." She tipped her head back to look around.

As long as she held onto the frame, she kept in contact with the attic and stayed locked into the timeline of Divine's Emporium and Neighborlee, Ohio. The winkies fluttered and sparkled in rapid strobing flashes, up and down the spectrum. The gossamer skin of the painting kept them from following her, just like it kept Maurice out when he was in his reduced form. Even though they couldn't cross over, Angela knew they could still hear and see her.

"Get help."

Chapter Two

"Best part of the day." Maurice sighed in weary pleasure and contentment and scooted over on the bench seat on the ferryboat's top deck. The engines groaned and made the boat shudder as it pulled away from the docks of South Bass Island. Behind them, the lights of the long slope down to the docks. Before them, the churning darkness of Lake Erie.

"Even though the wind is rising and the waves are getting bigger? And we're out in the middle of all that dark, cold water? And you can't swim?" Holly squealed when he pressed his lips against the ticklish spot under her ear.

"I warned you before. Torment the poor magic-less guy, you pay the penalty," he growled with unconvincing malice.

"I surrender!" She wriggled sideways on the bench. Maurice sat between her and the aisle, so all she could do was press closer against the railing and look over the side of the ferry at the water.

Maurice groaned in luxurious contentment, enjoying this mortal exhaustion, but not just because he knew it was as temporary as his full-sized body. He looked out over the dark, rolling expanse of the lake, trimmed by the lights of the mainland docks gleaming in the dusk in the distance. Evening had come far too soon. He wondered what sort of psychological explanation there was for the fact that the closer he got to the end of his two years of punishment, the faster the days of freedom sped by. Shouldn't the time slow down, like molasses in a winter that kept getting colder?

"Hey." Holly cupped his cheek. "I know what you're thinking."

"Nah. I mean, you spend enough time around magic, it starts to sink in and do things to your genetics, but no way you can read minds by now."

"Idiot." She mock-slapped his cheek once, a tap that told him how much she ached for him. "I know you're thinking about the time. We have a long drive ahead of us to get home, once we reach the docks. Too bad we have to spend the last of our day driving."

"If I had my magic, I could fold the distance and get us home in like five minutes. But if I had my magic, we wouldn't have the deadline."

"It's okay." She slid her hand around his neck, her fingers weaving through the curls that brushed the collar of his T-shirt. "We have all the time in the world in our dreams."

"Now you're the idiot, babe," Maurice groaned, and slid his arms around her to draw her up onto his lap. "I know how much it hurts you, knowing it's not real."

"Not as much as it used to when I thought I was insane." She sighed and let him cradle her, and nestled her cheek into his collarbone. "I can remember now. That makes all the difference in the world."

"I just wish... Sometimes I think I'd trade all my magic, permanently, to be able to be here with you full-time. You know?"

"Don't give up on magic just yet. Angela got you parole four times a year. She'll find a way for us to be together. I'm a Lost Kid, after all. There's got to be some magic in me, even if it's not active or visible or anything. That's got to count in our favor."

"Honey, there are all kinds of magic--believe me, 'cause I'm an expert--and I'll testify you have the best kind of magic of all."

"Uh, sorry." A blur of green and yellow sparks coalesced on the bench across the aisle from them and turned into Guber, one of Maurice's Fae friends who had decided to move to Neighborlee. Mostly to hide out from some lunatic fringe elements who wanted to force him to take the Fae throne. "Got an emergency over at Divine's."

"Like what?"

"We don't know, but the winkies came for every Fae in town, and we can't get into the building and we can't make contact with Angela." Guber shook his head, making his tangled hair fly, and his big brown eyes got bigger, sadder. "The protective net just gets nasty when we ask it to let us through. Like it doesn't believe we're friendly." He held out his hands. "Gonna be fast and kinda bumpy."

"Go for it." Maurice grabbed Guber's hand, and with his free hand reached for Holly.

She had spent enough time with him and learning about magic, she didn't need any prompting. She grabbed hold of his hand and Guber's.

"Here we go. Hold your breath and close your eyes if you get spacesick," Guber said with a grin.

Maurice was relieved when Holly obeyed right away, though there was no way she could be sure she got spacesick, since she had never been in zero-G and never traveled through N-space. Then he decided, since he was in a fully mortal, magic-less body, he might be smart not to take that risk himself. He closed his eyes just before the first kaleidoscope of electric green and red light reached out to grab him.

Ten seconds later, the light stopped leaking through under his eyelids and Guber let go. Maurice carefully opened his eyes and saw they had landed in the back garden of Divine's Emporium. Lori and Brick were there, and Bethany and Harry, and Lori's friend, Epsi, who was working with Guber on tracking down some problems with tainted chocolate getting into the Fae realms. Maurice reached out and caught hold of Holly, just before her knees folded. For a few seconds there was a fuss as he led her to the cluster of lawn furniture under the grape arbor that was just starting to get its first haze of green leaves, and got her seated on the chaise.

"Hey, where's the party?" Lanie Zephyr called, just before she wheeled around the corner, followed by her talented friends, Felicity and her husband, Jake, Kurt, Jane, and Daniel.

Maurice grinned when he realized Lanie's wheels didn't quite touch the ground, which was a good thing, because maneuvering the wheelchair through the damp, springtime grass would have been a struggle. Whoever thought of bringing them in had been smart. Whatever problem was keeping the other Fae locked out of Divine's might respond to non-Fae magic--if that was the right name for the talents Lanie and her friends possessed. They still weren't sure if they were from another planet, another dimension, another time, or really were escapees from a Nazi breeding experiment.

"Who called you?" Lori asked, as the group got situated in the chairs and on the grass, all facing the back of the big old Victorian house-turned-shop.

"Your little firefly friends got Stanzer and Dawn's trans-dimensional buddies all riled up. He's busy running down something touchy for a client and can't take off, so Dawn called and asked me to come check on Angela. So here we are. She's rounding up Athena and the computer gang, in case we need London's help." Lanie tipped her head back and narrowed her eyes at the tiny vent near the roof, where winkies slipped in and out in visible agitation. "Where is that?"

"You mean in the house, or where does that room lead?" Maurice asked. He knew he was splitting hairs, but that was part of the problem--something was making the hairs all over his body stand on end.

He hadn't thought he had any useful sensitivity to magic while he was in this condition, but some field of energy or magic or whatever it was came from the house in uneven ripples strong enough for him to feel it. A sense of discord grew louder. If it kept going, it might just make the roots of his teeth start itching.

"It's the painting room," Holly answered. "So what do we do?"

"We kind of figured since Maurice is assigned here, the net will let him through, even if it keeps everybody else out," Guber said.

"Makes sense." Maurice stood up and headed for the back door, his arms stretched out in front of him, just in case there was something magic in his way that he couldn't see. "Might want to get hold of Dawn if she's delayed and ask if the Hounds can try to get inside, if I'm no help."

"Double-team it." Holly struggled up from the chaise and followed him. She held out the teardrop-shaped opal that hung around her neck on a woven silk cord. It was her passkey to get into the shop, any time of the day or night.

"Brilliant." He wrapped his arm around her and kissed her cheek before they stepped up to the back door together. He wasn't afraid for her, if whatever caused the net to close and to cut Angela off from communication was still in the shop.

Holly might look like a mild-mannered, slightly plump children's librarian--which she was--but she had a wicked imagination and had been taking self-defense lessons since Christmas. That meant kicking and punching and using any weapon at hand, as well as understanding how to react to magic that might get thrown at her. After all, dating a Fae was almost a guarantee something weird would happen on a regular basis.

Maurice held his breath as they stepped up to the defensive net of magic enclosing the shop. It flared briefly, with a sensation like multiple pins jabbing all over his body and into his soul. Taking "samples" to identify him was the best description he could come up with for the sensation and activity. Rose and soft leaf-green light danced around Holly for a few seconds, and then the back door opened for them. Maurice didn't need to resort to the key Angela asked him to carry when he was in ordinary mortal Human guise. For instance, if he came home late at night and there was a police officer or someone else on the street to see him come in. There would be fewer questions if he had to use a key to unlock the door and get in.

He was relieved that he didn't need to use the key.

"Painting room?" Holly whispered as they walked through the back room, divided between Angela's gardening supplies and new items for the shop that had to be unpacked and assessed, and either priced or refurbished before going on the shelves.

"Painting room." He kept a grip on her hand as they headed through the shop and up the stairs. He walked before her. Just in case.

Maurice imagined he felt and maybe even heard the big old house breathing, relaxing a little as the two of them climbed higher. On the third-floor landing, he considered calling out to Angela, but common sense said if she was in trouble to the point that the defensive net of the house shut people out, then she probably wasn't in any condition to talk, or maybe even hear him.

Holly pointed to the right when they reached the landing with the door to the magic book library on the right and the door of the painting storage room on the left. Both doors were open, and that wasn't a good sign. Angela kept those rooms locked for a reason. Maurice nodded that he understood. The winkies had lit up the painting room, though, so he decided to go in there, first. Granted, there were some books in the inner, magically sealed room of the library that could cause problems if they were handled the wrong way. But Angela was up to taming any book, no matter how much inimical magic or how many inimical magical people might be stored in it.

Unless she had been hurt so badly by something in the painting room... No, he wouldn't think of that. He would concentrate on a positive image. Angela safe and laughing and a little embarrassed over whatever had happened.

The winkies circled a painting that sat on a crate near the

doorway. They kept trying to light on the frame and then flittering off again almost immediately. No wonder, Maurice decided a moment later, when he narrowed his eyes and separated the agitated red light of the winkies from the agitated red haze of magic coating the frame.

Then he saw the two hands gripping the bottom of the frame, the knuckles white and the tips of the fingers turning purple from trapped blood. He lunged forward, going to his knees on the crates, and grabbed hold of Angela's wrists. A hot sheet of irritated, strained magic wrapped around him, yanking the breath out of his lungs for a moment.

Angela looked up at him, pale and sweating, her lips bitten through and bloody, her eyes wide. Maurice nearly roared from the sudden stab of fear that cut through him. Angela's customary serenity was entirely missing--she was afraid and in pain.

"Hold on, Angie-baby," he growled, and threw himself backward, using all his weight to yank her up and out of the painting.

Holly shouted. Behind him, he was vaguely aware of running feet, thudding on the landing and then down the stairs.

Maurice gritted his teeth and leaned backward when the painting's magic got stubborn and resisted him. For a precious couple of heartbeats, Angela hung in mid-air, stretched between Maurice's hands and the painting, caught in it from the knees down.

At last, something snapped. There was a smell like ozone and hairs caught in a blow dryer. The two of them went tumbling toward the door of the painting room. Angela landed on him, her elbow in his gut, and Maurice saw stars when the back of his head hit the edge of a crate.

"You...okay?" he gasped, trying to convince his diaphragm to resume working and let him breathe.

"Maurice." Angela nodded. Sweat coated her face and darkened her hair. She closed her eyes and took a couple deep breaths. "Thank you."

"Hey, what are pals for?" Then he realized something was wrong. Missing. "Holly?"

"They took her." She staggered to her feet and past him.

Maurice turned over and got up, and saw the doorway and

landing were empty of Holly.

"Who?" He held out his arm and swallowed against a howl of anguish that wanted to come up his throat when she actually took his help to steady herself.

When did Angela need help from anyone?

"Whoever broke in. I've been thinking the whole time I was hanging there," she said as they hurried down the stairs as fast as her shaking legs would allow. "They came into the shop while I was still open for business and hid. Then something distracted me. Someone who understands magic got me to lose touch with the shop."

She let out a little snort when Maurice stared at her and actually came to a stop halfway down the flight of stairs between the third and second floors.

"Exactly." They resumed their flight down the stairs. "I was unbalanced enough by that, I didn't notice their presence until I did a full, conscious scan of the shop." Her legs were steady, and she had regained her normal color by the time they reached the ground floor.

The front door of the shop hung open. Holly stumbled back inside at that moment. She looked furious and unharmed. That was all that mattered to Maurice for a few heartbeats.

"They made me open the door for them!" Her shriek ended on a growl that made him think of the first time he saw her when he visited her dreams, dressed to play a Hollywood-style Robin Hood game. "Angela, are you all right?"

"They knew you had a passkey." Angela frowned and led the way to the main room, where the dimensional slits came open and released hot cappuccinos for them. "I was wrong again. They were prepared. Or else they knew enough to guess that was how you got in when they couldn't get out."

"Speaking of getting in." Maurice quickly explained how they had gotten back to the shop so quickly. In moments, Angela had released the protective net to let the other Fae and Lanie and her friends into the shop.

Lanie saw the first book, lying in the shadows at the bottom of the stairs, open and face-down, with its pages bent. Felicity hurried up the stairs and found another one that looked like it had been dropped during a hurried exit. Lori looked outside and found two more. While they were searching for more dropped books, Athena and Wallace and Dawn arrived. Maurice couldn't see the Hound that followed, guarding Dawn, but he felt its presence in the stinging sensation in the air. He tried to find some amusement in realizing that the physical reaction wasn't so bad when he was in his magic-less full size. Still, he was relieved when the Hound left, per their unofficial agreement of keeping distance from each other.

"So they were here for books," Angela mused, when everyone had settled down in the expanded coffee shop portion of the front room. She looked around the room and offered a crooked smile, blushing a little. "Thank you. All of you. It's been...quite a long time since I was the damsel in distress and needed some rescuing. Not a pleasant experience at all."

"The question is whether they got away with any books, or they were in such a hurry to escape they dropped everything," Bethany said. "Do you need help cataloging, checking what's there?"

"I won't know until I actually get up to the library and see how far they penetrated. But thank you."

Harry and Guber, who were talking about starting a Fae security and investigation business together, insisted on treating that night's incident in an "official" manner: going over the chronological sequence of events and taking test samples of the magical atmosphere; recording the magical resonance; and exploring the memory built into the protective net surrounding the shop, to see if they could get any clues.

Maurice realized how much the last hour had shaken him, when it struck him that ordinarily he would have made a few teasing remarks about how they conducted the investigation.

In the middle of it all, midnight came, and he was yanked away from the discussion, shrunk and squeezed back down to the five inches and wings of his exile. After spending the day as an ordinary mortal, the return of his magic, even though greatly reduced from his normal levels, was a relief that nearly brought tears to his eyes.

He flew around the shop, sinking halfway into the walls to get a taste of the magical resonance of the building, taking his own tests, gathering his own impressions. When he had done all he could think of, he settled down on Holly's shoulder to report to the others. He wasn't above admitting there was some comfort in the sweet strawberry scent of her hair, and the feeling of her pulse in her neck. Now that everyone was safe, he had time to feel terror on Angela's behalf, frustration at not having his magic available to help her, and fear that someday danger would wrap around Holly and he wouldn't be able to defend her.

~~~~~

Angela worked through the night, until past dawn, checking the library for any damage both physical and magical, and then checking the inventory. She worked her way in, from the least magical and alert books to the ones that had taken on a life of their own. Lori and Epsi insisted on helping her, along with Bethany and Holly. Dawn and Athena wanted to help, but they both had classes in the morning, high school and college. Angela wondered if they suspected she took on the task to avoid going to sleep and possibly dreaming.

She suspected now that last night's dream had been part of tonight's events. Either the dream had been triggered by someone testing her magical defenses or was a reaction to the new attack on the town's shield, or the dream had weakened and distracted her. The enemy, who had been watching all this time for such an opportunity, took advantage of it.

Bethany and Holly were the most help. Holly knew books, and Bethany had grown up in the shop, since Angela was her godmother. They were able to wade through the piles of books that had been toppled from their shelves during the thieves' search, pick up a book, and know its specific place on the shelves. That kinetic sense of memory helped shorten the time it took to identify which books were missing. Lori and Epsi concentrated on the protective spells enfolding the library. When they found a damaged thread in the protective net, they rewove and strengthened it. A side effect of that repair work was to let the books "go back to sleep," as Holly put it. They had been disturbed by the poking and prodding and picking of the intruders, and faint shimmers of magical dissonance sometimes rippled out of them during the cleanup.

By the time they finished with the outer library, Guber and Harry and Brick returned from Guber's workshop, with the components of an invention he had been tinkering with in response to a crisis in the Fae realms. As always happened when he worked on one problem, he came up with spin-off designs and applications.
~~~~~

With the help of the recording and filtering devices Guber had been refining, the plan was for Angela to look backward time-wise, to identify and see the books that had been stolen. By figuring out how the thieves had chosen the books they took, maybe she would be able to decipher what they had been looking for and what they wanted to do with the books.

They finished doing the scan of the outer library just after sunrise. Lanie and Felicity showed up with breakfast, and Kurt and Ford Longfellow arrived not long after with a burglar alarm they had spent the night designing for the shop. Angela was just tired enough to feel a rebuke forming on her lips. If magic couldn't protect her shop from intruders, what did Kurt and Ford, with all their mechanical abilities, think they could do?

Angela knew the answer to that question almost at the same time her tired mind and frayed nerves asked it. Kurt had a gift for making machines work when they had no right or reason to work. He had rebuilt a junker car during his junior year of high school, using all materials he had scavenged for free from junkyards. That car purred for him, and wouldn't even turn over for friends who borrowed it.

Lanie had told Angela about a time she, Kurt, and Felicity had gone on a picnic in the quarries north of the Metroparks. They were all in high school and middle school at the time, and her two friends were still living at the Neighborlee Children's Home. Whenever they thought they had developed a new angle to their unusual talents, they went to the quarries for privacy to experiment and practice. This time, some wannabe criminals scouting a new meth lab location had encountered the three teens and decided to frighten them to make sure they didn't cause any trouble. One of them stole the carburetor from Kurt's car, in an attempt to trap them. With Kurt driving, that car started up and sped out of there without any trouble.

"What are you going to do to your alarm to make it impervious to their magic, if they come back?" Angela asked Kurt, as he and Ford spread out the pieces of their newly built gizmo on the long table that had been set up in the main room of the shop for their breakfast. It occurred to her then--again late--that she should feel flattered and touched that the two of them had stayed up all night to build this for her.

"Well..." He shrugged, and colored a little, and glanced at his fiancée, Jane, who had just come through the door. "It's a passive system. With luck, it'll have so little reaction that these slimedogs won't know they've been spotted. We figured if they're using magic to blind you to their presence, they might not be looking for an old-fashioned burglar alarm. If you're warned, they can't zap you again."

Angela laughed, partly from weariness, and partly in amusement at herself for not having thought of that before. That was what friends were for, she decided, and delighted in kissing Kurt on the cheek and making him blush even darker. She was even more touched, to the point of tears--that could be blamed on exhaustion, though--when she learned that Kurt and Jane and Ford now had receivers set up in their homes, so they would know Divine's Emporium was under attack again, and they could come to help.

Lanie and Felicity finished setting up breakfast during Kurt's explanation of how the alarm system worked. It was heavy on hot chocolate and chocolate mega-muffins, in recognition of Fae dietary needs. Everyone gathered around in time to hear most of it. They immediately demanded their own receivers, so they could take turns being on the alert for Angela and Divine's Emporium.

Stanzer came in during the last part of this, with Dawn, who had decided this attack on Divine's was serious enough to justify skipping school. Their joining the group this late in the process required backing up and explaining what had happened and what had been found. Angela let Maurice and Guber do the explaining, while she watched Stanzer and Dawn.

She blamed the long night and the strain of everything that had happened, but only partly, for the feelings surging through her when she looked at Dawn and Stanzer. They had been betrothed as children, in another world, another dimension, before they were sent to Earth for safekeeping. Their dimensional guardians, the Hounds, had separated all the children by time as well as distance. Stanzer had been on Earth eight years before Dawn arrived, increasing the gap between them. Here on Earth, he was nearly thirty and she was a high school senior. The age and time difference constantly threw up barriers between them, and Angela sometimes wished she could knock some heads together--she wasn't quite sure whose--and order someone to have some pity or mercy or common sense.

Maybe her exhaustion made her imaginative, or maybe it tore down some barriers in her heart and mind and memory, but Angela felt an especially strong sympathy for them. As if, somewhere in her misty past, she had suffered the same kind of loss and separation and deprivation. Someone was out there for her, too, and she couldn't be with him. She knew she had a true love, her eternal destiny and soul mate, but was unsure if they had met and been separated, or he still had to arrive in her life.

If I dare go to sleep, will I dream of you? she mused, while listening as Stanzer and Dawn volunteered their skills in the search for the missing books and the thieves. The thought of perhaps seeing her true love, hearing his voice, and determining if he was real or just a wish-dream, was almost enough to drive away the uncharacteristic fear of dreaming that had gripped her more than a day ago.

~~~~~

By mid-afternoon, the middle and inner libraries had been searched and time-recorded. Both doors were locked, magically and physically, when Angela's team got to them, but they showed signs of having been attacked on both levels. It disturbed her more than she liked to admit, to discover the thieves had locked up after themselves. Did they have that much confidence in hiding their tracks? Or had it been the plan all along to toss her through that painting into a world that would eat her alive?

The middle library had less mess to clean up. The outer library was missing four books, and all the books that had been found in the wake of the departing thieves had belonged on those shelves. The middle library was missing eight books. Maurice opened the door of the inner library, and the magic released its usual shower of sparks as the seals were broken.

"As far as I can tell," he reported, after back-winging to land on the top edge of the laptop that controlled Guber's security and tracking gizmos, "nobody got this door open. They tried, but maybe they were still working on it when we showed up, and they ran."

"That's what I think," Angela said. "But better safe than sorry."

Only after they searched the room, which seemed to be exactly the way she had left it, did she admit she feared she had been wrong
~~~~~

in her assessment. And only to Maurice.

Guber's gizmos could go backward in time almost an entire day, getting images of the intruders and then backtracking them to show how they had come into the shop. The entire time, they had worn their black clothes and masks.

Angela found it odd that the thieves bothered to wear masks at all, when all the other customers in the shop who encountered them didn't seem to see them. Or at least they didn't react to them wearing masks and looking like refugees from a bad Ninja movie.

"My guess is that they had talismans from someone with some magic, to make them invisible. But either the people providing the talismans weren't sure they would work," Lori said, when she came to look at what Guber had found, "or the thieves themselves didn't trust them to work. Maybe they didn't quite believe in magic to begin with."

"Just add it to the things we have to ask them when we find them," Harry said with a sigh. He groaned, but cracked a grin, when an enormous list appeared in green and blue sparkles in the air above the computers he and Guber had labored over. A notation to "interrogate the creeps" appeared in Guber's very distinctive scrawl before the list winked out.

Dawn took over then, printing out and making electronic copies of pictures of the stolen books, taken from the images Guber had harvested magically and stored in his computer. She double-checked the inventory, ridding from her list the books that were still on the shelves, leaving only the titles and images of the missing books. She called in Athena Longfellow, whose talent included being able to find things on the Internet that no one else could, to search for places where the thieves might go with their stolen books.

They could have been hired by someone to steal the books from Divine's, in which case there might be Internet records of conversations in chat rooms or messages left on Internet message boards. Or they might have stolen the books to sell them, not knowing how valuable they were and how much real magic they actually contained. In that case, they could be on a multitude of bulletin boards for magic-users or even rare book dealers.

"The thing is," Dawn explained, "everything is on the Internet. You just need to know how to phrase the question properly or find the right triggers for the search parameters. Otherwise, you could be within a few bytes of finding what you need, and never get there. It's frustrating, I know from experience. Stayn and I are searching for the rest of the Hunt on the Internet." She glanced at Stanzer and something flashed between them.

"What?" Angela demanded. "Have you had some success?"

"We've...made contact," Stanzer said. "We're doing some research and following up, but they contacted us through the web site Dawn designed."

"So if inter-dimensional royal exiles can use the Internet, why not magic saboteurs?" Dawn said.

Angela had to agree. She hoped Dawn would find all the books on the Internet, on sale by and to people who had no idea what those books contained and what they could do in the wrong hands. Sometimes ignorance was a safeguard. The alternative was that whoever took those books knew exactly what they wanted to do and how to use those books, which meant they would never appear anywhere, not even in a vague reference to books stolen from a curiosity shop in the middle of the night.

When she went to bed that night, after being awake for almost two days straight, Angela had vague, innocuous dreams, and found she was disappointed. Dreams were her torment, yes, but they were also her clues and answers.

And this battle was not over. She sensed it had barely begun.

Chapter Three

"Maurice." Asmondius Pickle, head of the Fae Disciplinary Council that had exiled him to Earth a year-and-a-half ago, faded into view inside the Wishing Ball. "How are you, lad? Not getting itchy at this late date, are you?"

"Forget about me." Maurice snarled under his breath as his wings snapped into chop-and-liquefy speed. He clenched his fists and put all his control into calming them and folding them back out of the way. This was just another sign of how the pressure lately had messed him over. "It's Angela. I gotta know what's happening back home, and if it's coming after her."

"Coming after her?"

The Wishing Ball turned opaque, and then divided into two solid rainbow-swirled balls. One floated across the counter and over the edge, to drop to the floor and expand, while the other rainbow ball stayed in place and returned to normal Wishing Ball condition. The first expanded until Asmondius could step through it. He leaned forward, resting his elbows on the counter.

"What has been going on back home?" He leaned over Maurice for three seconds, then sighed and snapped his fingers, and vanished in a shower of sparks, to reappear standing on the counter, shrunken so he was eye-to-eye with Maurice. "That's better. What's this about something coming after Angela? I thought everything was settled once that doppelganger immolated on the town's shield. Don't tell me the rebel Fae have snuck back under our watch?"

"Who knows? The guardians and everybody slapped them down good enough, they should be licking their wounds and sulking for a couple years. The thing is, I figure with all the fuss over Mellisande dying and the anti-hereditary royalty loonies running around, and a bunch of different ministries hunting for who poisoned the chocolate, and figuring it came from Earth and carob-tainted chocolate, and taking so long to let Epsi out of the holding tank to help hunt and... Well, maybe some of the real extreme morons want to cut off all ties with the Human world." Maurice shrugged. "Can't stand Fae politics. It's even worse than what the Humans are going through, and that's saying a lot."

"Hmm, yes, there has been some upheaval lately. Can't say I mind, actually. Helps us pinpoint the troublemakers, cut out the rotten elements before they infect the whole, generate a new generation of rebels, that sort of thing. But I don't countenance our housecleaning spilling over and hurting our friends outside the Fae Realms." He snapped his fingers and two easy chairs appeared, with an oval table between them, loaded with chocolate cookies and pitchers of hot chocolate.

Maurice whistled, impressed. This was obviously going to be a long conversation, and Asmondius' knowledge about matters back in the Fae Realms made him ready to take Maurice's concerns seriously.

"Tell me what happened with Angela, first," Asmondius said, as they settled down in the chairs and poured their first cups. "She's been through more than enough trouble and sorrow down through the centuries, for our sake as well as her own sad history."

"She has a sad history? Like what?" Maurice sat up, nearly bobbling his cup before he took his first sip.

"Later, lad."

Maurice knew that frown meant business. Asmondius had been a family friend, and he had learned early to gauge the seriousness of the situation by the wrinkles on the elder statesman's forehead. Right now, he wagered he could scrub an entire football team's worth of socks on those ridges. Taking a deep breath, he gathered up his magic and shot it at the Wishing Ball.

Normally by this late in the evening, especially after all the work he had been doing, trying to help solve the mystery of the intruders and stolen books, he wouldn't have more than enough magic to turn on the protective net around the shop before he went to bed. However, the Wishing Ball was as aware as a centuries-old magical object could be, without having a trapped soul inside it, needing the kiss of a prince or princess to break the spell. The Wishing Ball cared about Angela as much as Maurice did, evidenced by its eager cooperation when he wanted to contact Asmondius for a serious conversation.

Now the Wishing Ball cooperated again, and the images of the night Angela was pushed through the painting flashed across its surface. Maurice nearly whistled his appreciation when the image split into four, showing different angles and vantage points in the shop, from late in the afternoon of the incident, up until he pulled Angela out of the painting and the intruders left the shop, using Holly to get through the magical protective net that tried to keep them inside. Obviously, the net and the Wishing Ball had been conferring, and they had picked up some tricks from Guber's monitoring gizmo.

Even with the advantages of fast-forward and judicious editing--also borrowed from Guber's gizmo--it took nearly two hours to show everything to Asmondius. All the hot chocolate was gone, and he hadn't hesitated to snap his fingers and bring in the really strong stuff: jars of hot fudge sauce, and spoons to eat directly out of the warmed jars. Maurice appreciated that, but this sign of how seriously Asmondius took all of this put off his appetite.

"There are a number of Fae living in this town now, are there not?" Asmondius said, after the images faded from the Wishing Ball, and he had continued to sit staring at the darkened surface for another ten, fifteen minutes. He didn't even look into the jar of hot fudge as he scraped the sides and thoughtfully sucked the spoon clean.

"Yeah. Angeloria--she's planning on marrying a Changeling, Brick. He's still learning the tricks. One of the descendants of the founder of the town. Then there's Harry, who's planning to set up shop doing investigations and inventing. He's settling down with Bethany, a local. She's got both guardian blood and Fae blood making things really crazy for her. She's been going back and forth between here and Hollywood, shutting down her career and dealing with crazies, but they're in town right now. Then there's Guber and Epsi. They're working on solving the whole poisoned chocolate riddle."

"Ah." Asmondius nodded. "That Guber and Epsi. Interesting that the whole mess with the throne and the anti-royalty extremists and the death of our Queen threw them together the way it has. I assume the magic of Neighborlee is working on them, as well?"

"Big-time, from what Lori says. Epsi's a total agoraphobe when it comes to the Human realm, but she's happy to be here."

"Love does wonderful things, lad." He winked. "Dare I assume you agree?" A chuckle escaped him when Maurice just grinned. "Anyone else to add to the list of considerations and variables?"

"Well, once we've got all the Fae listed, we need to look at the super-friends."

"The who?"

"No, they're on tour in..." Maurice grinned, not at all repentant at confusing Asmondius with his Human-cultural references. He had to be feeling better, to start making wisecracks again. "That's what I call all the kids in this town with powers. Not magic, actually. Of course, a lot of them aren't kids anymore, even though Lanie refers to them as the Lost Kids. They've been defending Neighborlee for generations. Angela calls them the guardians. You've met some of them when we were dealing with the problems with the lookalikes and the rebel Fae trying to break through."

"Ah, yes. I try to keep my visits to Neighborlee and my interactions with Angela's protégés as unofficial as possible. Otherwise, I'm compelled to write reports upon reports. I'm quite tired of all the discussions that resume whenever Neighborlee faces a challenge large enough to gain our attention. I have to be on the alert to discourage another proposal for a scientific expedition to camp here for a decade or two, to examine the impact of all the dimensional gates and slits and the non-Fae magic that seems to be as common here as spring water. Everyone with any sense knows that the simple act of observation has an effect on unusual phenomena. There's no control over whether that effect is negative or positive. We want Neighborlee to develop as naturally as it can."

"What's so natural about being a target for interdimensional invaders every year?" Maurice grumbled.

"True." Asmondius sighed. "Refresh my memory? I'm aware their numbers are increasing, and I'm sure I didn't interact with all of them when I was last here. We were rather busy unraveling those mysteries."

Quickly, Maurice ran through the list of the not-quite-Human allies in Neighborlee, and their gifts. Lanie, who retained her telekinesis after she broke her back and landed in a wheelchair. She also sometimes had flashes of future events and could tell if people lied to her if she touched them while they talked. Asmondius wasn't aware of those particular aspects of her talents. Mostly just her wry attitude toward life. Kurt had a gift for mechanical and electronic things, and the ability to "borrow" the talents of others. Felicity gave off EM bursts and had a talent for befriending and calling, at need, every dog within an eighty-mile radius. These three had grown up together, beginning life in the Neighborlee Children's Home.

The Longfellows were keeping guardian talents in the family. Ford was the patriarch, and the assumption for years was that his three children, Jinx, Lenore, and Portia, hadn't inherited any talents to become guardians. That was proven a false assumption when Portia's sensitivity to energy became a liability, with a strong chance of attracting a group of people who tried to steal Lost Kids just as their talents awoke. She had chosen to have a child and let everyone assume she had simply gone to a fertility clinic. The assumption was half-right: she had teamed up with Colonel Hayward, another Lost Kid, to have her daughter, Athena. Then when they realized that Portia's presence combined with Athena's was generating a resonance that would indeed alert and attract the Rivals, Portia had chosen to become a world traveler, seeking more Lost Kids, and left Athena for her parents to raise. In safety and anonymity.

Doni Longfellow was Lenore's daughter, orphaned at age nine. She didn't have any visible talents, but she was clever and part of the support team, along with her computer-genius boyfriend, Cosmo, Athena's fiancé, Wallace, and Jinx. Several other friends of the core group of guardians had grown in sensitivity over the years, after long exposure to the magic of Divine's Emporium. These included Gordon Priebe, a police officer, and his wife, Mandy; Troy and Diane Richards; and Gina Sinclair, the director of Eden, the community center.

Then there was Jane, Kurt's fiancée, who had been called the Ghost in the last town she lived in. Her gift let her phase out so she was invisible and could walk through walls and fly. She had been sent to Neighborlee by Hoax, Inc., the organization that had raised and trained her in her talents. They specialized in investigating and debunking paranormal, metaphysical, and simply unexplainable phenomena around the world. Usually, they covered up those odd events to protect the people at the core of them. Hoax was now an ally of the guardians of Neighborlee. Different members of Hoax came regularly to consult with Angela and meet with another group of allies who had come to town in the last year. The founders of Hoax were former Lost Kids from Neighborlee. They had spent the last few decades identifying Lost Kids before their particular talents manifested, to keep them safe from the Rivals and their willing minions, the Grandstone family, who wanted to enslave them and use their powers for evil.

A second group of allies to join the guardians were led by Arthur Sheridan, a Lost Kid who had built a communications empire. He had sent his grandson, Daniel, to Neighborlee to re-establish their family's roots and investigate the hints of odd and mysterious events over the years. Arthur still expressed some chagrin at having worked for so long in competition with Hoax's leaders and the guardians, to protect Lost Kids from the Rivals.

Then there were John Stanzer and Dawn Dover. They came from another dimension, and were looking for other refugees, whom they called the Hunt. Their interdimensional guardians, the Hounds of Hamin, manifested as big black dogs with silver eyes.

"Think that's enough to protect Angela from whatever's going on?" Maurice asked, as Asmondius finished taking notes on everything he had told him.

"We won't know until the time comes, will we?" he murmured, glancing over the tops of his thick horn-rimmed glasses. They had settled on the tip of his nose when the big notepad and quill pen appeared.

"Considering you know a whole lot more about what's threatening her than I do--"

"No, lad. That's the problem. It could be Angela's curse and her ancient enemies have awakened. It could be, as you said, dimensional invaders. They know Divine's Emporium holds together all the fraying strings of the... Well, let's call it the drawstring bag that keeps Otherness from popping through into the Human realm. There are many such spots throughout this world, and many Humans who have been recruited through the centuries to work with us and guard and hold everything together.

"The problem is that Earth is a nexus point. Many different dimensions and worlds converge here. Realities that even the Fae don't know about. It could be something even we can't see or touch or hear or smell, trying to come through here. Something is targeting Angela--or perhaps not Angela, but this house, this entire town, the gates physically anchored to this spot for stability.

"Neighborlee drips with magic and alternative-magical energy. That makes it a tempting target. It could be something or someone very nasty, who merely wants to absorb all the power and potential that has soaked into the very fiber and foundation of this place. These enemies couldn't care less about actually invading and dominating this world. That makes them even more dangerous than an enemy trying to take over, trying to use Neighborlee as a gatehouse to other dimensions."

"Why?"

"Do you care what damage you do to a bar of chocolate when you eat it?" Asmondius nodded slowly when Maurice swallowed down a surge of nausea at the mental image that provided. "At least with a magical despot, he wants to keep his new territory as much in one piece as possible, because he will need to use it in the future. Or in more mercenary terms, he wants to preserve as much profit as possible."

He sighed and put down the empty hot fudge jar. "Well, lad, I can't say I'm glad to have this to think about, but I am glad you were worried enough to consult me on this. We will put our heads together back home and see what we can do from our side of reality. You'll contact your friends and get to work on this?"

"You betcha."

A moment later, Asmondius vanished in a soft shower of green and blue sparks, taking everything with him except the plate of uneaten cookies and the fifth jar of untouched hot fudge sauce. Maurice smiled crookedly at that. Things had to be pretty serious for Asmondius to leave that for him. As in, provisions for a siege.

~~~~~

Several days later, Ethan Jarrod sat back in his creaking swivel chair and contemplated the notes haphazardly thumbtacked to the slightly grimy blank wall on the opposite side of his narrow office. He half-closed his eyes and let the disparate bits and pieces of his current investigative job mix and mingle in his subconscious, waiting for a couple puzzle pieces to slip together, for that flash of insight to make sense of unrelated bits and pieces and solve the puzzle.

An image rippled up to the front of his mind. *A house bathed in moonlight, with gables and narrow windows and flickers of sparks*
~~~~~

dancing along the eaves, surrounded by trees...

Muffling a curse, he sat forward, opened his eyes, and slammed his hands flat on his cluttered desk pad calendar. He reached for his cold mug of coffee. Why did those completely useless fragments of dreams keep intruding when he had work to do, important things to fill his mind?

They weren't memories. There was no gut reaction, no sense of recognition. Still, Ethan knew he would recognize the building again if he ever saw it in the light of day—and outside his dreams. Victorian, full of gingerbread trim, with gold and olive paint and a sign that read "Divine's Emporium." A sensation of warmth and welcome reached out, beckoning for him. He had awakened aching for something multiple times over the last few nights, but with no clues to help him remember what he had dreamed. Until now, when the fragments of his dream, like shards of glass, kept intruding into his work as a private investigator.

Too bad dreams never came true.

They used to, when he was a child. If he had ever been a child. What felt like centuries ago, he had thought he saw sparkling, winged creatures hovering at the edges of his vision. Sometimes he had heard them promising to help him and make all his wishes come true.

But there were some things even magical creatures couldn't handle. Hunger and loneliness and nightmares among them. Most of his past was darkness, his only memories of being alone and empty and hunting. It felt like multiple lifetimes.

Ethan had learned to ignore the whispers of advice and promises. Longer ago than he could remember, the colors and sparkles faded to nothing. Like his dreams of being a knight and rescuing his ladylove from dark bondage.

As always, if he ignored them and waited long enough, those bits of dream would fade and leave him in gloomy peace. That hurt, for the first time in years, but he was too busy for dreams.

Ethan retrieved the lost--things and people. To do that he had to triply focus his attention on reality. He exhausted his imagination, to the point that when he did dream, it was always related to work. Except for when those longing dreams intruded. This focus enabled him to put together disparate, unrelated clues and pieces to form pictures that solved puzzles.

He was good at what he did. Talented. Legendary. Some people even dared to tell him he had a magic touch. Ethan met their smiles with a cold, stony glare and silence and waited for them to change the subject.

He shoved the dream out of his consciousness and focused on his work. Another pot of triple-strong coffee, a few hours of working on the Internet, asking odd questions of strange connections, and an incipient headache helped free him of the disturbing interior interruptions.

But the recurring dreams of hidden passages and treasures, doors and windows that opened into other worlds, and toys that danced and played by themselves in the moonlight didn't fade and leave him alone as they had before, and that began to worry him. Six more nights in a row, Ethan ran through the big old house-turned-curiosity-shop, exploring and feeling like he still believed in magic and faeries and happily-ever-after.

The seventh night, *she* came into the shop and welcomed him with a smile. He knew her as if they had always been together. She said nothing, but he knew her voice was low and rich, sweet as honey and cream. Her hair streamed down her back and over her shoulders, to her waist, in a waterfall of gold and faint streaks of strawberry where the sun hit it just right. Big blue eyes gleamed like jewels. Not that he paid much attention to her eyes or her hair. He stood still for what felt like hours, staring at her mouth, trying to remember what those raspberry-colored lips tasted like, felt like against his mouth.

Ethan woke up aching and hungry in body and soul. If he didn't know better, he would have sworn his heart ached, but he had put his heart away years ago. It was the only way to stay safe. And sane.

His last open case resolved itself the next morning. The philandering wife he was following got into a three-way catfight with the wife and the girlfriend of her current lover. All three women ended up in the hospital. It would take months to determine who to charge with assault and who was the real victim.

Ethan's client, the suspicious husband, did a complete turnaround and went into white knight mode to protect his wife and put all the blame on the other man. He paid for copies of all the records of the past three months of investigation and to have them wiped from Ethan's records, plus a bonus for Ethan to lay low and pretend not to know what was going on if anyone came snooping. Plus, another bonus if he needed to testify in court, to turn his investigation into a defense.

Ethan took the money, promised to keep quiet and out of sight, and shook his head yet again at the obliviousness of some of his clients. Then he put it out of his mind. Long ago, he had come to terms with the ugly truth that he wouldn't be in business if people weren't self-blinded, foolish, overly idealistic, greedy, proud, and made a regular habit of doing the opposite of common sense. He solved their problems, found their lost treasures and missing puzzle pieces, without passing judgment, without getting personal even as he got inside their minds and souls. He was the best, recommended in whispers and innuendos and business cards discretely passed along, because he knew how to investigate without anyone realizing what he was doing, or sometimes even who or what he was chasing. It was almost as if he had magic at his disposal, to hide his presence and blur his footprints.

But Ethan didn't believe in magic.

With this investigation wrapped up, he needed something to occupy him. Not that he was worried. Work always seemed to find him before he had freedom to relax, read a book, or pay attention to the rest of the world. As if some power out there in the shadows worked to ensure he didn't know what was going on in the world.

Then John Stanzer called. Ethan had never heard of Stanzer, but something about the man's voice, the way he introduced himself and got right down to business, appealed to him. He agreed to look over the materials before he took time to investigate the man. The job sounded interesting. Old, rare books had been stolen and the owner suspected the thieves had taken them for the contents, rather than to sell and make a small fortune. Interestingly, Stanzer sent the materials by courier rather than as an email attachment.

The courier delivered the package of photos the next morning. By then, Ethan had investigated John Stanzer, P.I. He had a good, solid reputation. Nothing flashy, no run-ins with the law, until last summer, when he got tangled with a federal investigation. He came out of that with official thanks from the agents involved and a notation to contact Stanzer if anything with similar characteristics showed up again.

Ethan found it interesting that the records stating the characteristics of the case had been sealed. It almost piqued his interest, because he had access to federal records and files that many people working for that agency couldn't get into. What had Stanzer been involved in, besides helping to take down a notorious crime figure? Other than that blip, Stanzer worked quietly, with a reputation for being discrete and reliable, and refusing to take salacious cases. Ethan could respect a man like that. He had been like Stanzer once, trying to stay clean, honorable, helping only the helpless and downtrodden and abused.

But longer ago than he could remember, he had developed a need for intricate, tangled, dark cases to keep his mind occupied. Every step into the darkness brought him a little more silence, a little more numbing. The light had color and movement and whispers. The light brought dreams he couldn't remember when he woke, but his pillow was often damp with tears. Ethan chose to walk away from the questions that frustrated him, and sometimes laughed at the irony that he was afraid of his personal mysteries.

Because John Stanzer was the kind of man he sometimes wished he had remained, and because mysterious, esoteric books were a welcome relief from the usual cast list of embezzlers and kidnappers, blackmailers, frauds, and adulterers, Ethan was ready to take the case. He had a momentary spring in his step as he signed for the package, gave the courier a tip, and walked back to his desk.

Neighborlee, Ohio? Where was that? Ethan frowned at the return address on the label. He had been to every major city from New York to New Orleans, Los Angeles to Anchorage, and all the states in between. He had never heard of Neighborlee.

A chill he hadn't felt in years settled into his spine as he flipped through two atlases, then three road maps, then finally turned to the Internet. Why was it suddenly so important to pinpoint the town's location? It wasn't like he would go there when he found the books. Stanzer had already said he would come pick them up.

Ethan sat back, feeling that chill embed itself more deeply and stretch out tentacles from his spine into his gut and his scalp, when his computer slowed down in the search for Neighborlee on the Internet. That didn't make sense. He had access to the fastest search engines available. He should have his answers already on the screen in front of him, or the screen should give him a message that his request could not be answered, did he possibly mean something with a similar spelling?

The hourglass indicating "searching, please wait" kept turning over and over. He watched the indicator on his inbox rack up three more emails before the screen finally went white, then slowly scrolled down through his options.

Most of the offerings were online articles posted by the local newspaper, the *Neighborlee Tattler*. Well, that was a good sign. A place big enough to have its own newspaper wasn't a ghost town or a fake name on a false address. Sitting back and going the roundabout path, ignoring the wild goose and creating his own chase, had always yielded more and better results than the standard investigative pattern. Ethan opened up the website for the *Neighborlee Tattler*, and was pleased to see the menu offered access to their archives. A little more information on John Stanzer would be helpful.

An hour later, he had found several pictures of Stanzer from local events. He was involved in the Neighborlee Children's Home as a big brother, and acted in dramatic productions at a local church. An article eight years old introduced him to the community when he opened up for business there. Another article discussed his involvement with the local historical society when he bought and restored an old building and turned it into apartments in the middle of town.

"Well, well, you've had a few profitable years, haven't you?" Ethan murmured. He found it amusing that he hoped Stanzer had made his money by staying on the straight and narrow, instead of succumbing to the temptation private investigators faced, to profit from the very crimes they were being paid to prevent or solve.

Chapter Four

When he had read everything he could find on Stanzer, Ethan gave himself half an hour to investigate the town, mostly through the *Tattler*'s articles. He saved the Chamber of Commerce website for last. That was the face the local businesses and organizations *wanted* to present, which didn't necessarily equate to the real, honest face of the town. Of course, that didn't mean it was a false face, either.

He skimmed over information on the local college, the sports and academic honors for the Neighborlee School District, the local Metroparks, and crime statistics. It wasn't exactly Mayberry, but Neighborlee came across as a quiet, friendly little town where people knew their neighbors, ice cream trucks still roamed the streets, and children could walk to the playground in the evening without their parents worrying. The peacefulness of the town made Ethan wonder exactly why John Stanzer had set up shop as a P.I. there. Unless it was simply that there were no private investigators there until he showed up.

Ethan clicked on the Chamber of Commerce site and scrolled down the index, waiting for any business names or organizations that caught his attention. His instincts were always reliable, picking up and focusing on things that didn't make sense on first glance. A shimmer of light, a sudden stream of dust motes in the sunlight, a hint of a prismatic gleam, dragged his attention back to a button and a name--

His phone rang. Ethan snatched it up, his throat clenching in preparation for barking at whoever interrupted him.

No one there. Empty air, a few subliminal hums indicating the circuits were open. Then dial tone.

He put the receiver down slowly, wondering where that flash of fury had come from. He glanced at the clock in the corner of the monitor, and then at his inbox. Four more emails since he started reading about Neighborlee. He would give himself fifteen more minutes to soak up background before he opened Stanzer's packet.

And then he'd check his email.

Another stream of prismatic dust motes drew his attention back to a button on the Chamber's website. Ethan's hand trembled as he extended his finger to right-click the button. A whisper of high, childish, chiming laughter tickled his ears. He sat back, taking his hand off the mouse, and wiped both suddenly sweaty hands on the legs of his jeans. His office was on the eighth floor of the twenty-story office building and none of the businesses on his floor or the floors above or below him catered to children. So where had that laughter come from?

Ethan rested his hand on the mouse again and clicked on the button on the screen before he read it. A Victorian house done in gold and olive appeared on the screen.

"Stop wasting time," he snarled at himself, and his hand slid the mouse up to the red "x" in the corner of the screen, shutting down the page before it finished loading. Ethan cleared out of the search results screen and clicked on his email.

Ten emails waited for him. All looked like junk mail, the previews written in a language he didn't even understand. Some of the symbols looked like they were a foreign alphabet, but he could read the basics in Chinese, Arabic, and Cyrillic, and these symbols didn't even faintly resemble them. A flicker of anticipation, the pleasure he used to have in doing enormous, complicated jigsaw puzzles, washed over him. He reached to click the mouse button to open the first email.

More dust motes danced across his eyes. Instead of that high, childish laughter, he heard whispers. No distinct words, but the urgency in those voices made him shudder and sit back and rub at his temples, wondering what was wrong with him all of a sudden.

Hadn't he been worried about the time he had been wasting, just a minute ago? Why was it suddenly so important to open those junk mails and figure out what language they were in?

Ethan's gaze fell on the courier envelope, still unopened, sitting on top of his unnaturally clean desk pad. He had work to do, paying work, and that was what he should concentrate on. With resolute motions, he deleted the junk, closed down his email, and got off the Internet. Time to check that courier packet.

Just a few seconds of glancing through the contents of the packet gave him an even clearer image of the other investigator as a man who thought clearly and knew how to organize. Stanzer started by stating the owner of the books hadn't filed a police report because of the esoteric and secretive nature of the books. She couldn't file an insurance claim because she had no proof she had ever had custody of the books, and no one was supposed to even know she had the books.

Stanzer's report on exactly how the thieves had dismantled the security system was sketchy. Ethan didn't like that. It went against the mental picture and file of information he had already assembled on Stanzer. He found it interesting, and very telling about the value of the items stolen, when he read how the thieves had shoved the owner out a third story window. She had hung from the sill, so the other people in the building were focused on bringing her back to safety, leaving the thieves to make their escape unhindered. Stanzer included information on the books that had been dropped during the escape, as well as photos and descriptions of contents and the titles of the stolen books. Some didn't have titles--none written on their spines or covers. They could only be identified by the diagrams drawn and dyed or cut into their ancient leather and wood covers.

A prickle of unease traveled Ethan's back and up into his scalp as he studied the photos of the stolen books, taken from surveillance camera footage. The images were grainy, probably low resolution to begin with, and blown up.

Why didn't the owner have photos of the books already in her files, if they were so valuable? That was on the top of the list of questions Ethan asked in a voicemail message for Stanzer.

"The easy answer is that the contents of the books are so dangerous, Angela didn't even want to have photos of them lying around," Stanzer said later that day when he called back.

"Dangerous how? Dust containing anthrax? Samples of the bubonic plague?" He choked back the next words, stopping himself just in time when he realized he was about to say, "evil magic spells."

"These books belonged to some pretty nasty people in the past," Stanzer said slowly, making Ethan think he knew the whole story and was editing as he went along. He could respect that. He had done the same for his clients, who had trusted him with treacherous information but depended on him to protect them.

"Combine the Borgias and Vlad the Impaler with the worst movie sorcerers... "

"Sorcerers? Come on. You can find all kinds of nasty spell books in any New Age shop. Just because people believe in it doesn't mean it's real." Ethan put his feet up on his desk and frowned at the sudden shifting in the shadows of his office. That didn't make sense. The shades were down, blocking out the afternoon sunshine altogether.

"Yeah, well, mixed in with all the spells and curses and mumbo jumbo, there's some pretty nasty real stuff. Poison, stuff that makes modern chemical warfare seem like pepper spray."

"Okay. I get what you're trying not to say." Not quite, but Ethan was used to playing word games to protect his clients. He found it interesting that Stanzer's client, Angela, worried more about what someone would learn from the books than about the value of the books themselves as antiques. Then again, the contents might have historical value, maybe even damaging historical impact. Like a document proving a royal pedigree was false, or a hero had been at home on the day of his career-making battle, or that Hitler hadn't committed suicide and he was living in Brooklyn with Eva and doting on twenty great-grandchildren.

When he got off the phone, Ethan had a plan of action roughed out in his head. He wouldn't look for the books themselves. They wouldn't be on the market. He agreed with Stanzer and Angela's fear that the books had been stolen for a specific purpose or person. Stanzer's description of Angela's security precautions and the setup of her library confirmed that the average cat burglar or drug addict thief wouldn't have been able to find those books. Only someone who knew the books existed and Angela had them could imagine the security precautions to be circumvented, and where they might be hidden.

That meant Ethan would start his search by looking for the people who wanted those books. His trips into the darkness and the Dark Web had netted him contacts and sources of information and networks that people went to when they were in the market for the strange and dangerous. The people who wanted Angela's books wouldn't do the stealing. They would hire professionals. Ethan would go to the marketplace where those professionals communicated with prospective clients. If his theory was correct, he had a narrow window of opportunity to catch the communication between the thieves and their clients, announcing the job had been done, and making arrangements where to meet to exchange the stolen goods.

~~~~~

"We might have them," Stanzer announced, bombing through the front door of Divine's Emporium just before closing, a week after the break-in.

"Who? The thieves or their boss?" Maurice swooped in from the front room to meet him. He settled on a shoulder and held onto his collar as Stanzer hurried into the front room.

"We think the thieves." He grinned and wiped sweat off his forehead.

"But?" Angela nudged the Wishing Ball a half-inch to the left. "And who is 'we'?"

"Another P.I. I'm working with. Ethan Jarrod. He has quite a rep for finding the un-findable. People, things, doesn't matter." With a foot, Stanzer hooked one of the tall stools tucked against the wall and dragged it over to the counter, to sit down. "He's setting up a meet with them very late tonight. If I leave in the next hour, I'll get there just in time."

"And do what?" Maurice wanted to know. He hopped down off Stanzer's shoulder and onto the counter. "Beat a confession out of them?"

"Mostly likely you'll be able to scare a confession from them, if they stole the books for someone else, and they get a glimpse of what's under the disguise," Angela mused.

"Hey, Angie? You're getting kind of scary."

"Maybe I should have been scary sooner." She shook her head and offered them both a flicker of a smile.

"Whoever wanted those books, they're up to no good. They know enough to work around your safeguards," Stanzer said. "You think maybe it's the same people who blackmailed Troy last year, to steal that book? Maybe Kerri has come back for round three?"

"That's what I hope we find out. And I hope they're not the same person."

"Why?" Maurice jumped up, fluttering his wings to hover for a few seconds before landing on the top of the old-fashioned brass cash register. "It just means we have more enemies here."
~~~~~

"True, but the book that our enemy tried to steal last year is of a very different type than the ones stolen last week. Different implications. I would much rather it be two different people, two different forces, than one enemy able to reach in different directions and dimensions."

"Makes sense. Kind of like Gahlmorag turning out to be that thing Lanie and the others ran into at Eden." Stanzer's face grew more somber.

Maurice whistled softly in appreciation. Gahlmorag was the enemy Stanzer and Dawn and the rest of the Hunt were hiding from, and were expected to return home to fight someday, when they had found each other and joined forces. Stanzer had described him as: *A galactic despot who gobbles up planets by enslaving the ruling families. It's a bonus if he can enslave people with talents. That's why the Hunt is here on Earth, growing up and learning to use our talents, instead of on our home world.*

The idea that Gahlmorag was already on Earth and had been causing trouble in Neighborlee for years shook Maurice more than he wanted to admit.

"Anyway, I thought it might be smart to get some insurance," Stanzer continued, and thumped his fist on the counter for punctuation. "Want to come along?"

"Oh... I'd like to, but I don't want to leave the shop alone," Angela said. "Not when those thieves left behind so many books. Whoever hired them might send someone else back."

"I'll go," Maurice said, resisting the urge to jump up and down, waving his arms. This was too serious for his usual foolery. "Hey, I'm small but mighty. And I haven't used much magic at all today. Got lots of ammo, just in case."

"Maurice, would you?" She leaned down toward him, bracing her arms on the counter. "I would appreciate it immensely."

"Anything for you, Angie-baby."

~~~~~

Maurice decided Stanzer had a nasty joker streak that he didn't get to show very often in his line of work. For the first hour of their journey east, they earned quite a few odd looks from people passing them on the highway, who saw Stanzer talking and laughing with apparently no one in the car with him. When it was safe to take his gaze off the road, Stanzer turned his head and
~~~~~

maintained eye contact with the passing drivers or their passengers, his expression innocent or alarmed. The mask cracked as soon as the other car sped away. He and Maurice laughed, sometimes so hard the car swerved in the lane.

Half an hour from the Pennsylvania-New York line, they turned off the highway to get burgers and coffee. Stanzer suggested they actually go in and sit down to eat, and made a wager on how long it would take someone to notice the half a burger hovering a few inches off the table, slowly vanishing as Maurice ate it. For a few seconds, Maurice considered taking him up on it. He liked how the P.I. thought.

"How are we doing for time?" he asked instead. He choked a moment later when it occurred to him that he was acting a lot more responsible and mature than usual. Maybe it was the seriousness of the threat and mystery facing Angela, or maybe it was the growing pressure of wondering what he and Holly were going to do when his exile ended, and he regained his normal size and magic levels.

"Yeah, didn't think of that." Stanzer didn't sound too disappointed. He pulled into the drive-thru lane instead of parking. "I'd be interested in finding out if Jarrod can see you."

"What makes you think he would?" Maurice hopped out of the seat that had been rigged for him so he could see out the window-- essentially a paper cup with chamois lining, hanging from the headrest of the passenger seat. He flew to land on the dashboard underneath the rearview mirror.

"His rep. A lot of close calls, some conflicting testimony when things went sour during an investigation, but he came out smelling like a rose. He seems to specialize in weirdness, if you know what I mean."

"Things that would be a lot easier to understand if there was some magic involved?" Maurice chewed over that idea while Stanzer pulled up next to the speaker and placed their order. "So, what do we do if he does see me? How you gonna keep the guy from freaking? I mean, I'm not that easy to explain without a playbook," he said, once they had their order and were on the road again.

"We'll deal with it when the time comes. Sometimes that's the best way to approach everything and anything in life. Just relax and see what happens. You get a lot fewer ulcers."

"Yeah, but it gives the dragons a chance to sneak up on you and take your head off," he muttered. Maurice could hardly keep a straight face when Stanzer glared at him. Then a few moments later, they were both laughing. Wry laughter that didn't last long.

Ethan Jarrod waited for them in the parking lot of the municipal center, containing a city pool, baseball diamond, soccer field, skateboard park, library, and mini-golf course. Half the tall lights were either burned out or went off with timers to conserve electricity at 4a.m. Maurice went up for a bird's-eye-view reconnoiter as soon as Stanzer parked. He found the man waiting in the shadows of the bleachers, just as arranged.

"I think I have your answer," he said, dropping down to land on Stanzer's shoulder. He gestured with a lift of his chin toward the dark, man-shaped blot on the edge of the baseball diamond.

Only a dark blot for those who couldn't see or sense magic.

"Whoa," Stanzer said, barely keeping his voice soft. "No wonder the guy seems kind of sour on the phone. I'd be ticked to have those things hanging around me all the time. Gotta make it hard to sleep."

"Yeah. I feel for him." Maurice muffled a snicker, but at the same time he did feel some sympathy for the other P.I.

Winkies swirled around him like a swarm of killer bees around their queen. They spiraled in and out, creating a cloud of neon light in streaks of pink, green, yellow, and purple. Oddly, the little magical fireflies never landed on the man who stood there, arms crossed over his chest, watching Stanzer walk toward him. He didn't wave away the winkies, didn't even blink when little blobs of light spun up toward his face and back out again.

Which, now that he thought of it, Maurice found rather odd. This Ethan Jarrod had to be a man of infinite patience, because the presence of that many winkies would have driven Maurice crazy long ago. He'd have been investing in fly swatters and the strongest insect repellent he could find in the Human and Fae realms.

Either Ethan didn't care...or he couldn't see them.

"Could be," Stanzer murmured, when Maurice posed his theory. Then they were in the shadows of the bleachers and Ethan was extending his hand.

Maurice studied Ethan as the two private investigators exchanged information and finalized their plan for confronting the thieves. Hovering in the air only six inches from the man, he felt a faint itching in the magical atmosphere. Like sand. Or maybe sandpaper was a more accurate description? And heat. Ripples of it. After a good ten minutes of observation, he picked up the pattern. The winkies didn't land on Ethan and they swirled away from him when the hot, itchy sensation in the air grew stronger. The man was generating whatever repelled the winkies.

"Wish you could have taught me that trick a couple centuries ago when I was a kid," Maurice said, flying in close enough he could have landed on Ethan's shoulder. "You know how my big sister and my mom kept an eye on me? Winkies. Everywhere I--"

Ethan's head snapped around, and for a second Maurice was eyeball-to-eyeball with him. That big blue, bloodshot eye narrowed. Maurice fluttered back away from him, swallowing down the rest of what he was going to say.

"You think the guy heard me?" he said, coming in for a landing on Stanzer's shoulder. He didn't expect an answer, since the two of them were too busy conferring. Stanzer could do a lot of things, but talking mind-to-mind wasn't one of them.

He stayed on Stanzer's shoulder as the two men got in Ethan's car and drove around the municipal center to the darkened corner of the lot next to the swimming pool. The reek of industrial-strength cleaner in the warm air, as the city prepared the pool for filling, made him cough. It amused him a little to see Ethan look around several times, and then scowl and make a visible effort not to hear.

"The guy's got a lot of anger, and he's using it to fuel his own brand of personal shields, guess you'd call it," he speculated aloud to Stanzer. "He doesn't see what he doesn't want to see. Kind of makes me wonder how he got his reputation, if he's choosing to be blind."

Stanzer let Ethan get ahead of him a good dozen yards. "Look at it this way," he whispered. "Someone who can put up a shield like that without knowing what he's doing--that's strength and discipline. Not somebody I'd want to hack off at me. Know what I mean?"

"Oh, yeah." Maurice ached for a smart remark, to ease some of the tension that rippled through him and made his wings itch. But he couldn't think of a single thing to say.

He kept silent when the three figures dressed all in dark clothes came out from behind the snack shack next to the pool. He wanted so badly to snark about them wearing the same clothes since breaking into Divine's Emporium, but he didn't think it wise to distract Ethan. If these were the ones who had broken in, they had pepper sprayed Angela and tried to shove her through a painting into a pretty unfriendly alternate world. They knew how to deal with magic and weren't afraid to be nasty about it. Chances were good they had brought guns. Or more pepper spray.

Maurice knew how to deal with that, at least. He wasn't in the mood to try to deflect bullets. Like Angela often said, preparation was worth ten times as much as innovation.

"Hey, fellas," he said, concentrating on the winkies swirling around Ethan. "Want to help out the good guys here?"

The trio didn't react to the light show swirling around Ethan, meaning they couldn't see the winkies. However, if they had some rudimentary training in dealing with magic, maybe they could *feel* when a tornado of winkies wrapped around them.

While they were distracted, Maurice planned to do a little recon.

Stanzer flinched and opened his mouth to say something, then stopped himself when the winkies arched up away from Ethan, and then swirled around and down. They reminded Maurice of the way the dragon in the first *Shrek* movie pounced on the villain. Ethan blinked, scowled, shook his head and kept talking to the trio.

But they weren't listening. All three yelped and twitched away from each other and looked around. Definitely, they *felt* the magic at work. They were all maybe in their early twenties, just kids trying to look and act tough. They looked scared as they flinched and twitched and stepped out of the shadows into the dim light, then back into the shadows. Over and over. Maurice watched for a few seconds as the winkies wove in and out through the black clothes to bite and scratch and tickle. Then he dove at the first suspicious-looking bulge tucked into the waistband of one pair of jeans, in the small of the spokesman's back. It took some doing, but he yanked up the heavy black T-shirt and exposed the gun, despite the twitching and flinching of its owner. His own personal bucking bronco. Maurice thought he might be seasick by the time he got a firm grip on the butt of the gun and flew up and away.

Stanzer glared at him and stepped around, trying to get behind the three twitchers and Ethan, to take the gun from him. Maurice saluted him, two fingers flicked off his eyebrow, and dove back into the growing whirlwind of thieves and winkies. They were getting louder. Ethan scowled more.

"What's wrong with you? Are you high?" the other P.I. demanded, grabbing hold of the shortest one's shoulders.

"Good job, pal. Thanks." Maurice dove down to tug up the T-shirt on this one while he held still. "What's wrong with you guys? Everybody has to dress alike and hide their guns in the same place. This is the last of them," he added as he pulled the gun out.

He broke free as the kid let out a yelp and turned, scrabbling at his back with one hand and reaching for the gun with the other. Maurice turned a somersault in mid-air--not that easy, even with the help of his wings--and flung the gun Stanzer's way.

Ethan caught it, his scowl so deep Maurice thought the grooves in his forehead and around his eyes had dug in permanently. The three thieves let out shrieks and cowered back into the shadows.

"Hold it right there, kids," Stanzer said, and drew the gun Maurice had given him.

"He said it wouldn't follow us. Honest, we were just doing a job. We didn't mean anybody any harm!" the tallest one whined, while putting his hands up in the air.

"What wouldn't follow you?" Ethan snarled.

"There is something just plain freaky about that place we robbed to get those books you wanted. We don't want nothin' more to do with the place or the guy."

"What guy?" Stanzer stepped closer.

The three yelped again when the winkies formed a hollow pillar, enclosing them from head to toe in a swirling of pink and green and gold sparks. Maurice grinned when he caught the angry humming of the winkies. He suspected some of them had caught the news from whatever information sharing network the winkies used. They recognized these three as the ones who had broken into Divine's Emporium and pushed Angela into the painting. Winkies protected their friends.

One thief let out a shriek and went to his knees, pressing his hands over his eyes. The sting of pepper spray wafted softly through the air. Yes, definitely, the winkies had identified them, and returned the favor, returning the pepper spray to the one who actually shot Angela. Winkies were kind of scary at times, but Maurice was glad they were on his side for once.

"What guy?" Ethan echoed and stepped forward. The muzzle of his gun almost touched the swirling wall of winkies.

"Where are the books?" Stanzer said.

"Here! Take them. We don't want them. Couldn't get rid of them anyway." The middle one wriggled free of his backpack and tossed it through the wall of winkies to Stanzer.

Ethan and Maurice stood guard while Stanzer opened the backpack and turned on the slim flashlight he kept in his back pocket.

"That's three of them. You took eight altogether from Divine's Emporium. Where are the others?"

"We got rid of them right away. The guy paid us and was pissed we didn't get all the books he wanted. He only paid us half what he said. Told us to sell these books to make up for messing up." Fear barely gave way to sullen tones.

Maurice considered asking the winkies to tighten their walls around the three prisoners. He doubted they were going to get anything useful out of the thieves if they were scared enough to mess their pants. Besides, there was the stink to deal with.

Ethan and Stanzer took turns snapping questions at them.

Maurice hovered several feet away, out of the orbit range of the winkies, to watch and listen, and admire their skill. The two P.I.s had never worked together, but they were a good team, ratcheting up the pressure, changing the angle of the questions, getting the three to stumble and contradict themselves as they slowly wrung the details out of them.

Their employer had contacted them through the Internet. He'd met them in an abandoned warehouse, staying in the shadows. He had provided them a shopping list and drawings of the images on the covers and inside the pages of the books he wanted. He gave them charms and talismans to wear, to help them get through the safeguards of Divine's Emporium.

From the way the hapless thieves talked, they didn't realize what they had gotten involved in at first. Then odd things started happening, like people not seeing them when they did some early reconnaissance of the shop a week earlier. They actually thought the bits of metal and wire they wore short-circuited the burglar alarm and cameras inside the shop. Then they got inside Divine's and the shop started to defend itself, reacting to the attack on Angela, and they had realized Divine's Emporium wasn't their normal breaking-and-entering, snatch-and-dash job.

"They're definitely wasted," Ethan said. "Look at them. Probably hallucinating right now." He gestured at the three punks, pressed close together, shivering, twitching whenever a winkie did a diving run at them.

"Doesn't mean they aren't telling the truth." Stanzer glanced at Maurice, then tipped his head toward them.

"Ease up?" Maurice guessed. When Stanzer nodded, one corner of his mouth twitching up, he made a mental image of what he wanted, and then focused on the winkies. "Thanks, guys. Job's almost done."

The walls of the prison slowly eased outward, giving the thieves some breathing room.

"They're useless," Ethan said. "Your client still hasn't filed even a basic police report, has she?" He sighed loudly, and his scowl deepened when Stanzer shook his head. "Won't do us any good to drag these three all the way back to Ohio, then. No authority to do anything here, no charges to file with the locals."

"What do you suggest, then?" Stanzer said.

"Think anybody'd notice if they just vanished?" He turned his head so that only Stanzer, and Maurice by default, could see his wink. "Clean up the place a little. Bury the trash, y'know?"

"Hey," one of the punks yelped. "We didn't--"

The tall one bent within the relaxed confines of the prison of winkies and snatched a knife from his ankle sheath. Black and purple light flared from the knife. For a split second, Maurice could have sworn it dragged the kid after it, leaping through the air at Ethan.

Stanzer shouted and whipped out the gun he had just put in his pocket. He fired into the dirt at the punks' feet.

Ethan cursed in a language Maurice only vaguely recognized. He spun, kicking and punching, ducking under the arch of that blade that trailed poisonous black and green light. The spark of purple light at the blade's tip flared, almost blinding, but it missed Ethan's shoulder and scorched through his jacket. Ethan punched up with one fist, then the other, tossing his attacker into the air with the force of his blows. More light exploded, separating Ethan and the kid.

The knife went flying.

Winkies and Maurice raced to catch it.

The winkies won. And lost.

Maurice came to a screeching halt in mid-air, which was only possible with magic. He stared as winkies touched the knife and erupted into flames. They screamed and half the cloud vanished altogether, flittering back to whatever dimension birthed them. The knife tumbled end over end, shedding a cloud of burned winkies and a trail of foul-smelling smoke, before clattering to the asphalt.

When he turned around, Maurice saw Ethan sprawled on his back. His attacker had curled up, wisps of smoke drifting up from his body, maybe ten feet away. Stanzer stood over the other two punks, who cowered on their knees with their foreheads to the pavement and their arms over their heads.

"You okay?" Stanzer glanced back at Maurice, but kept his gun trained on the two still-conscious thieves.

"Yeah. How about you? How come the big bad wolfies didn't show up?" Maurice decided he would have welcomed some interference from the Hounds of Hamin about now. He caught a whiff of burned winkies and fought not to choke and heave.

"My life wasn't in enough danger." He shrugged, baring his teeth in an attempt at a grin. "How's Jarrod?"

Maurice shook himself free of the repeating images of winkies bursting into flame and flew over to land on Ethan's chest and check his vital signs. Before he could do more than listen to the rhythm of his heartbeats and make sure his chest rose and fell with breathing, the big man groaned and put a hand to his forehead. His eyes flickered open.

"Stanzer?" Ethan groaned.

"How you feeling?"

"Like I went a dozen rounds with a guy who had bricks in his gloves." He sat up, rubbing his face with both hands, and looked around, blinking rapidly as if his eyes wouldn't focus. "What happened?"

"I'm guessing he had a Taser or something nastier, maybe black market. You got a couple blows in before he got you. What do you guys think?" Stanzer gestured with his gun at the two whimpering thieves.

They just whimpered louder. It sounded to Maurice like they were begging the two P.I.s not to hurt them.

When Ethan was on his feet again, he and Stanzer took care of securing the unconscious one and then his buddies. Maurice kept watch on the knife, but he didn't want to get too close. If anybody showed up to try to take it while Stanzer and Ethan were getting their three prisoners to Ethan's car, they were welcome to it and whatever problems it caused them.

The problem resolved itself before Stanzer could break away from Ethan and come back to the spot. The blade of the knife rippled like it was starting to melt, and then evaporated before Maurice's eyes, with tiny hissing sounds and flickers of purple and black light. The haft remained, ebony and silver, but it had a transparent look by the time Stanzer bent down to touch it with one finger. He hissed and jumped back, started to put his finger to his mouth, then paused and wiped it on his jeans instead.

"What do you think it is?" he asked Maurice.

"Nothing I ever dealt with before," he hated to admit. "Don't suppose your Gahlmorag dude specializes in this kind of stuff?"

"Not that I know of. Should we hope Angela knows what's going on, when we tell her about it?" Stanzer stood up, wiping his hand on his jeans again, as the haft of the knife faded away altogether. The spot where it lay looked like it had been scorched, the bare dirt melted by intense heat.

"She's scary enough as it is without having this kind of stuff in her brain." Maurice shuddered. "How's the big guy?"

"He'll feel better when he takes care of the trouble triplets."

"Think he was just kidding? You know--about making them vanish? Burying the trash?"

"Hope so." He leaned back, bracing his hands against his hips and stretching a little. "Ready to head home?"

"Sounds good." Maurice flew over and landed on Stanzer's shoulder. "Think Angela'll have any answers about Ethan?"

"I don't know. He can feel magic working. He blocks the winkies by force of will. Who knows what else? But the question is if he's conscious of it or not. And if not, why not?"

"Whatever's going on, this guy is bad news for somebody."

~~~~~
~~~~~

Ethan found more amusement in Stanzer's reaction to his suggestion that they bury the book thieves than in the fear the three punks showed. It bothered him a little that they couldn't find the Taser or the knife when they searched the area. He put in a call to a friend in the local police department, letting him know what had gone down in the early morning hours and to be on the lookout for the weapons to appear--or anything else unusual.

"Story of my life," he muttered, his mind tripping over the word "unusual."

Lately, weirdness and "unusual" had been cropping up a little too much in the investigations he conducted, almost as if he was a magnet for the bizarre and slightly unreal. Pushing it out of his consciousness took a little more effort lately. On the other hand, he was getting better at it, able to sense the unworldliness tiptoeing into the room behind him, so to speak, long before it could be heard or smelled or seen. Then he would concentrate, focus, push it away, and it would be gone again. Until the next investigation.

Ethan took the three blindfolded and whimpering thieves into the lake district and drove as far as he could into the forest, then hauled them out and marched them until sunrise. He left them deep in the woods with strict instructions not to move. That would hold them for maybe fifteen minutes, he figured.

The sound of the forest waking up for the day covered his retreating footsteps. The punks would eventually get frightened or nervous enough to make a stupid move. When nothing happened, they would get a little braver, until finally they would work around the ropes on their wrists to remove their blindfolds and find themselves alone in the middle of nowhere. They were in a section of forest that wasn't regularly patrolled by the park service, so it might be a whole day before the threesome stumbled on another human being. Or maybe they would find the road and have the sense to follow it back to civilization.

Chapter Five

What they did after that, how they got back to their home territory, was entirely up to them. Ethan hoped the scare they got would slow them down. He didn't have much hope for a change in their minds and attitudes. Long ago, he had tried to talk sense into some of the hoodlums he had encountered. The ones who laughed at him and scorned his advice were much more honest than the ones who seemed to listen, who agreed with the observations he made about their lifestyles and promised they would change. And then didn't. Ethan had given up on trying to help, so long ago he couldn't remember when it had happened.

He returned to his office around lunchtime, put a call in for his friend in the police department, filed a report on the case, and left a message for Stanzer to see what his client's reaction was. Then he leaned back in his chair, closed his eyes, and the dream swallowed him before he took another breath.

He stood inside a castle courtyard. Everything was moonlight and shadows and decay. The stonework on all sides crumbled where it wasn't covered with moss and ivy. He crossed the courtyard, up the tall steps, through the double doors that hung open, the wood rotting so the hinges had fallen into piles of rust on the cobblestones. The darkness parted before him, revealing the grand hall with its roof open to the sky. In the spill of moonlight, he made out blurred shapes that could be mistaken for men.

As he got closer, he saw the vines and moss covering the shapes, and the glimpses of bare bones and scraps of fine cloth, swords, rings, and necklaces. They had once been men and women. What had caught them, freezing them in mid-stride? What kept them upright when they should have fallen into piles of detritus ages ago?

A shadow moved, up near the roof. He looked up, and realized he looked through a helmet. Raising one hand to touch the helmet showed he wore heavy metal gauntlets, once shiny silver but now spotted with the same mold and rot that touched everything else in this castle. He shuddered, imagining looking into a mirror and seeing he was nothing but a bare skull trapped inside the helmet.

The movement resolved into a woman, standing in the doorway of the gallery above, braced against the cold, moon-bleached stone. She stared down at the scene of death and decay, her eyes wide, her mouth open in a soundless cry of dismay. The moonlight turned her heavy gown with long, draping sleeves to silver and gray and white. The only warmth and color in the scene came from the heavy gold of her hair and the blue of her eyes. Her skin was as pale as the moonlight enclosing her.

Her gaze met his and she staggered, nearly stumbling forward, off the rotted remains of the gallery. He took a step closer to her, making the skeletal figure on his right sway. Soft, silent dust rose up in the air, and slowly, the figure toppled. It hit the one behind it, which also swayed and toppled, hitting two more, as the air filled with silver-white dust that formed clawed hands, reaching toward the woman who stared at him, tears glistening diamond-bright and sharp in her eyes.

Ethan gasped and sat upright, yanking himself out of the dream.

He reached for the phone like a lifeline. It rang as his hand touched it. He gladly dove into whatever mundane questions a prospective client might have for him. Only later, when he went home exhausted and headachy, did he pause to wonder if his panic and the force of his will caused the phone to ring.

As night closed in, and sleep approached, he thought about the dream and wondered if he would see the woman again. There was something familiar about her, a sense of warmth, of completion. Ethan supposed if she was a product of his imagination, then he could have dreamed of her many times.

That was the logical explanation. He lived his life by logic. Even though right now, there was something very sad and empty about logic.

<center>~~~~~</center>

The next morning, the Von Helados came into Ethan's office to discuss a missing person they needed desperately to track down.

"It's for her own good, of course." The slim grandmother who led the delegation spoke in a delicate voice that couldn't hide her grim Iron Maiden determination. She wore unrelieved black, as did the four men who accompanied her.

They stood over her like sheltering oaks. Oaks that had been charred in a killer forest fire and stayed standing, protecting the delicate plant resting among their roots.

Nightshade, Ethan decided. She acted delicate but had more power and deadliness than all four escorts combined. She tried to look brokenhearted but couldn't mask the glint of cold anger in her eyes that made Mafioso bosses look like jolly clowns at the circus.

"Why is it for her own good?" Ethan used the quiet voice that never failed to make his clients sit up and look closer at him.

The four turned their dead black gazes on him, and stepped a little closer to Iron Grandma, as if they thought he could be a threat.

"Dearest Annabelle isn't quite right in her head. She's harmless. So very good-hearted. And that's the problem. She sees herself as a good faerie, helping everyone who crosses her path. There are horrid people in this world who would take advantage of her."

Yeah, and I bet she has mega-bucks and you want to make sure she doesn't give that money to anyone but you, Ethan mused.

"This will help you," Mrs. Von Helado said. She opened up her iron black shoulder bag and brought out what Ethan thought was a large coin. Round, with a dull gleam, a little bigger than a half-dollar piece. It hung on a chain of fine black beads interspersed with silver links.

"How?" He didn't hold out his hand to take the coin, so she had to put it on the desk between them.

For just a second, Ethan's stomach twisted and all his muscles tightened in preparation ... for what? For battle? For flight? For violent sickness that would empty his insides across the desk?

He had the oddest sensation that he had sat facing this same woman many times, in different rooms, different clothes, different cities and countries, each time with that coin gleaming dully at him. The scene always ended as he took the coin.

He wasn't going to touch it.

He inhaled, managing at the last moment not to sound like he had taken his first breath in days. The scene steadied in front of him, and he shoved away that momentary flight of dark fantasy.

"Annabelle wore this constantly as a child," the woman said on a sigh. Her eyes bored into him. He suspected she was irritated she had to explain this. "She loved it. I hope that when she sees it, she'll see you as a friend and trust you, and let you bring her home."

"Why don't you just go see her yourself?" Ethan tapped the papers the youngest Von Helado had put on his desk. One was a pencil sketch of innocent, demented, lost Annabelle. The other was a list of possible places to find her.

"We don't want to frighten her, of course."

Ethan muffled a snort. If he were on the run, he'd take off at first sight of this troop dressed like a bunch of undertakers.

"Annabelle vanished during a fire at our family mansion. She believes our ancestral home was destroyed and our whole family is dead. That sent her running the first time we found her. We don't want to send her into hysterics again, showing up on her doorstep without warning."

"So when I find her, I show her the coin, make friends with her, get her to go for a ride with me and bring her home." Ethan had heard much more cockeyed plans in his career. Against all odds, some of them actually worked. "You think if she sees the house is all right, she'll figure out everyone is okay and come running home for milk and cookies."

"Succinctly put, yes." She nodded.

A glint in her eyes let Ethan know she didn't appreciate his stab at humor. That was fine. He didn't like anyone in the grim group on the other side of his desk. He didn't have to like his clients. Or trust them. The need to rescue innocence drove him, to solve mysteries and find the lost. The paycheck was far down the list.

When the Von Helados left, Ethan listened for the sound of a car pulling away on the street below his open window. Through the normal sounds of the city in the mid-morning slump, he heard nothing. So, they were rich enough to afford a new, luxurious car with a quiet engine and hinges that didn't sound like a gunshot. That didn't mean they really cared and Annabelle truly was a demented soul. Ethan tried not to pass judgment, just get his job done and find the truth. When he found Annabelle, he'd know both sides of the story.

He caught up the chain with a pen, to take a closer look at the coin. Gut instinct, not that momentary mental wandering that could easily be blamed on low blood sugar, warned him not to let the chain touch his bare flesh. Not yet, anyway. Not until he got it tested for poison or drugs.

The coin had three flattened spots on the edges, equidistant, so Ethan knew it was deliberate and not an accident. The metal didn't look old or dirty, so much as it had a reddish cast, a dull film that obscured the surface. His fingers itched at the thought of touching it. What had Iron Grandma tried to foist on him? To hurt or control poor Annabelle? Ethan had an instant vision of Annabelle snatching up the coin, delighted to have a childhood memory back, only to be drugged on contact.

Then again, this whole scheme might not be about Annabelle at all, but an elaborate revenge aimed at him. It had happened before. He was very good at what he did. Uncomfortably good. When he helped innocents, he made enemies of their oppressors. Such people sometimes felt it necessary to try to eliminate the one who had been their victim's champion. Emphasis on "try."

The Von Helados had paid in cash. They wanted as little record as possible, claiming it was "to spare poor Annabelle the embarrassment." People who didn't want records or a paper trail had things to hide. Von Helado could even be a fake name. The only way he would get answers was to find Annabelle.

Ethan turned the coin over, using his letter opener. He couldn't make out what was on the back. Someone had slashed it with something sharp, gouging the surface before it got the red coating. What had been there and why had it been defaced?

~~~~~

He dreamed of the Victorian house again that night.

He couldn't get through the door to go inside. The angel with gold and strawberry hair and sea-blue eyes appeared on the porch. She smiled and beckoned for him to come inside with her. He took a few steps forward, wanting to go in, aching for it as painfully as he longed to taste her raspberry-colored lips.

She spoke to him, but he couldn't hear her. She held out her hand and stepped backward. One foot rested on the threshold. Strangling panic shot through Ethan. If she went inside without him, he'd never find her again. He caught hold of her hand and pulled. Hard.

The woman screamed and he heard it, with his ears and deep in his bones. She tried to pull her hand free. He gripped with both hands and pulled back, away from the house. Her face went white with panic and tears streamed. They hit his hand and burned him. Ethan pulled harder. She screamed, louder, higher, breaking only to sob. He pulled harder, with a massive yank as if he'd tear all his muscles. She stumbled forward, into his arms.

Silence.

She stared into his eyes, barely managing to keep her head up when her whole body went limp. Ethan cradled her against his chest.
~~~~~

"No. Please," she whispered.

Ethan paused and looked back at the house. It had vanished into mist. When he looked at her again, he nearly dropped her.

She faded before his eyes. All her luxurious gold and strawberry and blue-green turned to gray and black. She shriveled into a pale, wrinkled crone in the matter of a few heartbeats. Her eyes went dead black. Then she turned to dust, disintegrating out of his arms.

Ethan woke drenched in sweat, heart racing and aching as if he'd been kicked in gut and chest and spine.

"It's just a dream." He scrubbed his hot, sweaty face with shaking hands. He didn't believe in dreams.

A high-pitched sound, like a child's shrieking giggle, floated through the stifling quiet. Ethan's studio apartment windows were open and the curtains drifted in the breeze, but the air around his bed was still and thick and heavy. He heard no sounds from outside. He felt surrounded by invisible watchers, all holding their breaths, waiting for him to do something.

"I don't need this," he muttered. "If I'm going to have crazy dreams, I might as well start drinking myself to sleep."

Flickers of gold and emerald and blue danced at the edges of his vision. Daring him to look. Sweat poured down his back and forehead. Ethan refused to look. The high-pitched burst of childish laughter turned into a sigh. The colors faded. The air returned, cool and fresh and moving again.

Ethan stretched out on his back and closed his eyes. He didn't sleep, and he was honest enough to admit he didn't want to sleep.

If he had any friends close enough to confide in, they'd tell him to take a vacation, that stress brought on the hallucinations. Ethan knew better. The more work he took on, the busier he kept his mind, the sooner the dreams would go back into the closet in his mind, and he would have peace.

~~~~~

Angela sat in the dark in her kitchen and sipped cold tea and listened to the night. All was well in the sleepy college town. The deer in the woods crept through the spring mist or lay in their sheltered spots and waited for day. Owls fluttered to their nests. A soft, cool breeze meandered through the park and up the slope to Divine's Emporium. It brought her the scents of sleeping flowers and pine trees, budding maples and oaks and elms, the sharp
~~~~~

perfume of cut grass that had baked all day in the warm spring sunshine, and dust churned up by a few local boys violating curfew on the park roads. All was well. Except inside Divine's.

She had dreamed four nights in a row now of the knight in mottled silver-gray armor that shifted in color with the play of moonlight across its surface. If he was silver turning black, or black turning silver, she didn't know. Angela only knew if she could get him to come into Divine's Emporium, they would both be safe.

Tonight, she had been a fool. Angela understood dreams and dreaming and knew they had more power over reality than most people could ever believe in the light of day. She had never before been helpless in dreams. Tonight, the dream had caught her up and carried her along. When the gray knight appeared, she had dared to believe she could coax him into the shop. She stepped across the threshold, and thereby lost all the protection Divine's Emporium wrapped around her, day and night, waking and sleeping.

He caught hold of her hands and fire shot through her veins. He pulled her off the porch, into nothingness. His armor burned cold against her skin. The metal bit into her flesh and drained her life, shredding her soul. Panic nearly destroyed her control.

Just before she tore free of the dream, his armor melted away and she saw part of his face. Dark, curly hair, stern, lightless blue eyes, and a wide, hard mouth. Angela was sure she would know him if she ever saw him in the daylight, just by those few details. She would know him by the chill up her spine, the burning cold in her flesh, and the warm, hungry churning in her belly.

She had no memory of feeling that aching, sweet need before, yet the sensation felt familiar all the same. If this man was a tool of her enemies, they might well have found the one weapon, the one weakness in her wisdom and strength, that could destroy all the secrets and treasures Divine's Emporium guarded, and Angela herself.

"The funny thing is," she told the darkness, her sheltering friend, "I would enjoy it. I have to die sometime. Why not die happy?"

Sparks coalesced out of the darkness, turning into winkies, all light and wings, sparkles and high, sweet, whispering voices. They danced around her, living shards of rainbows. They didn't speak, but in their song and the patterns of their dancing flight, Angela understood their concerns and pleas and soothing promises.

"Don't worry. It was just a flutter of self-pity. Nothing more. I won't give up." She closed her eyes and fought the heat and damp filling them that threatened to become tears.

~~~~~

The next morning, Diane and Meggie Richards came into the shop. In one week, they were heading to Paris with Troy, Diane's husband and Meggie's brother. He was attending a summit on hazardous material handling. The women would do the tourist thing while he was busy, and when the summit was over, Meggie would come home, and Diane and Troy would take a vacation.

"He actually had the sense to call it Honeymoon Part II," Meggie said, cupping her hands around her mouth and speaking in a stage whisper, as if confiding some incredible secret. Diane just laughed.

"So we need some spiffy duds," Diane said, after Maurice flew in to join them and had to be updated on the story. "We know the vintage clothing room by heart. Do you have anything that hasn't been put out yet, maybe?"

"I have just the thing," Angela said. "You'll make those stick-thin models hanging out in Paris bloat up and turn green with jealousy."

On the way upstairs, she envisioned the perfect dress for Diane and called it into being. Perfect for a second honeymoon with a man who adored her as much as she adored him. Calf-length, creamy white, cap sleeves, with tiny blue flowers dotted all over the lacy overdress. Diane fell in love with it the moment she walked into the storage room. She didn't see the dress that hung on the dressmaker's dummy at the back of the room.

That dress hadn't been there before. Angela had dreamed of that dress once, with long, draping sleeves and scooped neck, gold embroidery and tapestry on the hem and cuffs, like a lady would wear to Camelot. She had put away the dream decades ago. Why had it re-emerged now to taunt her?

Angela thought of the knight in her dreams and shivered. For the first time in decades, she felt a twinge of envy as she listened to Diane chatter about all the things she had to do before the Paris trip. Later, when Maurice was busy with Guber, investigating a shipment to the Fae realms of carob-contaminated chocolate, which
~~~~~

was lethal to some Fae, Angela went back upstairs. Just to see if the dress was still there, or if it had evaporated, once again nothing but a bittersweet dream.

The dress was there, but the colors had faded and the embroidery looked worn in spots. As if she had worn it often since she first dreamed of it. If she had worn it, why didn't she remember doing so?

She went into the painting room and checked to see if any of the images there had changed, indicating changes in the worlds they touched. A chill passed over her as she approached the painting she had fallen into during the robbery, and she paused to study it. Again, she wondered: Had she fallen totally by accident, or had it been planned? Who had hired the three foolish young thieves and given them instructions and tools to break through the magic guarding Divine's Emporium? Had he chosen that painting and told them to aim her into it, or was her fall truly just bad luck, happenstance?

"Are you home?" she whispered, and flinched, taking two steps backward.

Why had she asked that question? Why had she even thought it?

Now that idea stuck in her head. Was it possible that one of these paintings was the doorway to the world she had originally come from? Was she even less Human than she thought? And if she had come from another world, another level of reality, what would happen if she stepped through?

Would nothing be changed? Would she be able to return to Earth, to Neighborlee, and Divine's Emporium? Because no matter where she originated, this shop, this town, this spot on Earth, was her home now.

"Stop it," she scolded herself, and swept out of the attic. For good measure, she pulled the door closed with a solid bang and ran her index finger around the handle three times, effectively sealing the room. She didn't like sealing anything inside the old house, because doing so interfered with the currents, both physical airflow and magical. But until this unknown enemy was caught, a little extra caution would be wise.

Coming back downstairs, she was surprised to see the light had changed more than she thought, indicating it was later in the day. Had she lost time again? Angela paused on the landing between the third and second floors and looked out the side window. From one angle, she saw the slope down to the Metroparks and the bright afternoon sunshine. The sun sat lower in the sky than she thought it should be. Double-checking, Angela turned around twice going right, then turned around once going left, while standing on the second step above the landing. Now the view changed through the same window, showing her a thick forest heavy with oaks and moss. No sunlight could penetrate the canopy there, and the time of day was measured by the changing colors of the winkies that encrusted everything that didn't move. Right now they were magenta with a hint of purple, meaning the day headed toward evening.

How had she lost track of time?

"Losing track of everything," she muttered, and considered contacting some friends in the Fae realms, to come give the shop and her a long-overdue examination. Maybe she had brought some magical illness back with her from that unplanned tumble into the painting. She had already lost some of her serenity, now her sense of time was failing her. What would go next?

Lips pressed flat together in concentration, she reversed her turns, to take the window to its normal, Earth-linked view, and continued down the stairs. At the second-floor landing, the wallpaper shimmered, the lavender and gray print darkening momentarily to give her the impression of high stone walls with an ornate silver gate, and a shadowy garden beyond the gate. The moment she stopped to look at the image there on the wall, it faded back to the abstract wallpaper pattern. Angela kept walking and rubbed her arms against a chill that didn't come from the air, but from deep inside her.

What if... What if all this that she knew here and now was a dream, and the shadowy garden was her reality?

"Don't be ridiculous," she scolded herself as she headed down the stairs to the main floor. Still, it would be wise to consult friends with more knowledge and skill, and much stronger magic.

The sound of voices in muted conversation, coming from the front room of the shop, surprised her, because she sensed no other bodies in the building beyond herself and Maurice. She hadn't sensed him returning from his errand, until now. That was another sign of how long she had been upstairs and how much time she had lost. Angela reached with her sense of magic, trying to determine who was here.

Definitely no other living bodies in the shop besides herself and Maurice, but there seemed to be an inordinate amount of energy vibrating around the Wishing Ball. Frowning, she stepped around the corner. Her gaze landed on the ball and she nearly laughed aloud in relief when she understood.

"Well, Asmondius, to what do we owe the pleasure?" She stepped up to the counter where Maurice sat on a pile of paperbacks, facing the Wishing Ball. Asmondius stood about as tall as Maurice, inside the ball doing duty as a communication globe at the moment.

"Angela. You're looking well." The Fae administrator and liaison between Divine's Emporium and the Fae government nodded and exchanged a glance with Maurice that Angela could only describe as "meaningful."

"All right, what are the two of you up to?" She settled onto a stool behind the counter.

"Maurice asked me to check on things here, just in case all the recent unrest might have anything to do with your latest problem."

"He did?" She tipped her head to one side, fighting not to laugh or even smile when Maurice flinched and then sat up straight, meeting her gaze with an almost defiant one of his own. Angela sighed. "Thank you, Maurice. I should have thought of that myself. What's the verdict?"

"Time has been slowing down incredibly on this side of things, probably as a result of all the tension. Only a few days have passed here, compared to weeks on your side. I've only started the investigation, but right now we're still focused on tracking down the source of the chocolate that killed Queen Mellisande."

"Yeah, and I was telling him the theory Guber and Harry and some others have been tossing around, trying to help Epsi," Maurice offered.

"The reactionaries are too busy trying to place blame on the anti-royalty contingents, as well as the extremists who want to re-establish a hereditary throne. If they decide to blame the traffic between the Human and Fae realms, it could be months in our time, maybe years in yours before the decision is made to limit or even cancel all access between realms," Asmondius reported. "All the same, it might be wise to make contact with all the Fae you know are living in the Human realms and give them warning. Start considering their choices and options if the door is ever shut."

"I'll do that. Thank you." Angela began mentally listing all the Fae on Earth with whom they were in contact. She made her farewells with Asmondius and got up to pull out a notepad and pen, to write down her ideas. This was something serious enough that she couldn't risk forgetting one name or connection.

"Hey, Angela?" Maurice fluttered over her shoulder as she settled down at the little wrought iron table to get to work. "What happens to Divine's if the doorways get closed?"

"I like to think there's so much magic embedded in these walls, we won't even notice for years that the air and currents from the Fae Realms no longer touch us." She looked up from her list and met his gaze. Something tightened in her chest at the concern wrinkling his face. "Did you ever think that cutting access down to a bare minimum might be good for you?"

"Heck, they can cut off anything they want, as long as I'm on this side of the door with Holly." He offered a brave smile and fluttered down to stand on the table, one foot resting on the top edge of her notepad. "Will you be okay?"

"I think so. It will be interesting to see what changes, what slits into other realities close up altogether, and which ones are harder to keep closed when the...well, when the air pressure changes, so to speak."

"Yeah, there's interesting, and then there's irritating interesting. Think problems like Big Ugly might wake up again?"

"That very well could happen. And doorways we never felt before might awaken, without the calming influence of the protective spells placed on this house. All the magic could flee altogether, leaving me an ordinary woman in an ordinary shop. Who knows?"

Angela's thoughts flickered for a moment to that glimpse of gates and shadowy woods, hidden among the wallpaper on the second-floor landing. Was that another world trying to break through, make contact? An illusion? Or a gate that should have been sealed for all time? With all the upheaval and disturbances in magic in the multi-realms, were the wards wearing down and threatening to let that other reality break through?

One thing at a time, she told herself, and bent her head over the list. There were many Fae who would choose to stay in the Human realm, if the easy access to the Fae Realms was narrowed down or halted altogether. She could depend on them to help her defend Divine's Emporium, to keep control over the doorways into other realities and dimensions. Or at the very least, they would help her destroy the place, sealing all the openings once and for all.

~~~~~

Ethan worked for two weeks on the list of leads the Von Helados gave him. Everything came up blanks, and he was relieved to be able to call them at the end of the probation period and tell them so. Something about them awakened all the caring and instincts he had put away for years, making him feel involved with the search for dim, lost Annabelle.

Problem: he didn't want these people to find her. Ethan offered the Von Helados the option to end their contract, pay him only for the time expended, and they could go on their way to find someone else. To his surprise and disappointment, they claimed to be very pleased with what he had done so far, eliminating so many leads. They gave him another list of possibilities, more towns where they had hints of Annabelle's presence. Despite his instincts getting tangled up with unwanted emotions, Ethan took the job.

He set up a map on the blank wall in his office and put blue pins in the places he had investigated, and green pins in the places he had to check out. Something twisted in his gut and stole his breath when he stepped back from that chore and saw a circle clearly delineated on the map. He moved in closer, eyeballing the center of the empty spot in northern Ohio, close to Lake Erie. Another shiver made the hairs on his arms stand up as if he had been struck by lightning. Neighborlee wasn't printed on that map, but he knew it sat in the center of that empty circle.

Ethan put that observation aside for later and made his plans to investigate the new set of leads and information the Von Helados gave him. That decision was taken away from him when leads on one more book stolen from Stanzer's client came up. He followed them, and within two days got the book off an Internet site.

Instead of calling Stanzer to come meet him and pick up the book, Ethan listened to his gut instinct and prepared for a road trip.
~~~~~

He wanted to see this town, and the woman who owned such unusual, rare, possibly dangerous books. He wanted to know why she chose not to have insurance or a documented inventory, and not to have the police involved when her shop was broken into. Neighborlee, Ohio, couldn't possibly be like the picture presented in the online bits and pieces. There had to be something odd about a town that barely appeared as a flyspeck on the map, and only seemed to exist to give the local college a mailing address.

Just before he left his office to hit the road, the lab sent back the report on the coin Mrs. Von Helado gave him. It was silver. The discoloration was partly blood, partly an alchemist's warehouse of herbs. There were no poisons or electronic devices embedded in the coin or the chain of onyx beads, but the lab did report low-level radiation that grew weaker with time. The experts felt the radiation was so low-level, it should cause no harm or make any noticeable changes in the wearer over the long term.

Ethan's mind stumbled over the "should" part. Low-level radiation? He dismissed the images that sprang to mind, fed by B-grade movies. Gut instinct made him check the sky and the phases of the moon on his calendar. Nearly full moon, waxing to full. He wondered if the radiation would grow stronger as the moon waned again.

"You're going bonkers," he scolded himself. Ethan had no idea where he got the notion of the talisman's power being linked to the moon. And when, exactly, had he begun thinking of it as a "talisman"?

Maybe he was losing his mind. But on the plus side, for two weeks, he hadn't dreamed of the angel who had shriveled to dust in his arms. Ethan knew he was better off without dreams.

So why did he feel more tired and less satisfied every morning he woke up without any dreams behind him?

Chapter Six

When he got to Neighborlee, Ethan took a room in a small bed & breakfast on the edge of town and set about getting to know the place, the rhythm and heart. He strolled around town for two days, getting the feel of the town and letting the locals get used to his presence. Just like hunting in the forest, all he would get was silence until he became a semi-familiar face, talked to people, proved he was an ordinary guy, and gained some acceptance in the environment. He talked to shop owners, librarians, and rangers on patrol in the park. He walked around the campus of Willis-Brooks College, watched the baseball and soccer teams practice, and admired the Century homes and lush lawns and gardens.

Late afternoon of the second day, he saw the sign for a private investigator's office in the front window of a six-story building on Long Street. Stanzer's office. He felt a pang of envy, seeing the old-fashioned building, the perfect, picturesque location, and wished he had been there first and thought to settle and open his own office. Right there.

Ethan was carrying the stolen book with him, just to prevent it being stolen again, so he had no excuse to delay the reckoning. He walked up to the recessed doorway and stepped inside. The door was propped open and a fan helped circulate the warm summer air. He used to dream of having a place like this. Old-fashioned, shadowy, relaxed, like in the movies.

"Can I help you with something?" a man asked out of the shadows. A moment later, Stanzer stepped through the connecting door from the next room. He laughed. The welcome on his face as he held out a hand to shake made Ethan feel a little guilty, a little uncomfortable, and yet strangely glad.

"Nice place," Ethan said after he handed over the book and they settled down at Stanzer's desk with bottles of iced tea. "I envy you. Been walking around, getting the feeling of the town. You have the perfect setup. If it wasn't so quiet, so pretty, I'd be tempted."

"Move to Neighborlee?" Stanzer nodded slowly, his expression thoughtful. "There's more action around here than you'd think."

"Looks are deceiving?" Ethan felt his interest perk up. Nothing like talking shop.

"Neighborlee is a great place. It's the surrounding towns that keep me busy."

They talked for maybe twenty minutes, slipping into the easy semi-familiarity that only came from a deep well of common experience. Quirky cases, changes in the law, cooperation or the lack of it from local law enforcement, guns, and changes brought by technology.

Ethan was pleased to see Stanzer used some of the same methods he did, including big maps on the wall with pins, notes and pictures tacked up to try to get the bigger picture. It reminded him of the Von Helado case, which he had gladly put on hold for a few days to tend to the stolen book.

"Give me your take on this. I have these clients, looking for a missing relative. The leads they've given me are all over the place, from one coast to another. Except when you make a map and mark all the spots, what *isn't* included in the hunt is really obvious." He gestured with his bottle of tea at the map on Stanzer's wall. "There's a great big gaping hole where they either don't have any information, or maybe they don't want anyone to look. And at a rough guess, this town is pretty near the center of where I shouldn't be looking. Makes me wonder..."

"Like maybe there's something about this town?" Stanzer shrugged. "There's a lot about this town, but if you don't have the right mindset, it can drive you nuts. Maybe I can help, since this is my home territory. Anything odd about this missing person? Anything to start from?"

"Bare bones. She's supposed to be helpless, unable to deal with reality, and has a tendency to run away. They have strange instructions for how to approach her, if I ever do find her. Which made me leery of getting involved in the first place."

"But you did anyway."

"Curiosity." He reached into his coat pocket, pulled out the folded copy of the sketch of Annabelle, and tossed it to Stanzer. "There's something about her picture. For one thing, why a sketch and not a photo? I just can't put my finger on what it is."

"That so?" Stanzer's smile didn't change when he opened up the paper, but Ethan felt tension shoot through the office.

Something dropped into his stomach. A heavy mix of dread, disappointment, and anticipation. "You know her?"

"The woman I know is far from helpless or unable to deal with reality." He continued to stare at the sketch. "These people claim she's a runaway?"

"They say she got lost when there was a fire at the family estate, and she's so out of it she believes everyone is dead. She freaked the last time they caught up with her, which is why they hired me, to break the news to her gradually, I suppose."

"Too familiar ..." Stanzer's expression seemed to close up. He sighed and rubbed his forehead. "I dealt with something like this a couple months ago. Another P.I. came in here, looking for a runaway teen. It was a scam, trying to get their hands on a girl I'm protecting. Now you show up with this sketch and that story..." He sighed. "I should warn you, we protect our own in Neighborlee."

"I'm not here to make trouble. Just wanted to drop off your book."

"Maybe not, but trouble's what you'll get if you do anything to harm Angela."

"Isn't that the name of the woman who owns the books?"

"One and the same."

"I don't believe in coincidences, do you?"

Stanzer slowly shook his head, his gaze assessing and weighing Ethan. Then he inhaled sharply, and he visibly came to a decision. "The only way we're going to figure out what's going on, what the link is between these people and this sketch and Angela-- and maybe the robbery a few weeks ago--is to ask questions."

Ethan felt that tightening in his gut, the tensing of his scalp, the tingling in his fingers that had warned him long ago of... The only word he could come up with was "otherness." But he had lost that sense of otherness back in the darkness, back when he had learned to be logical and orderly and ignore the gaping holes in his past and most of his personal life.

He didn't argue when Stanzer asked for his promise not to do anything but ask questions, and not to reject anything he might see and hear and feel for the rest of his stay in Neighborlee. Ethan promised, quickly. That sense of otherness deepened, as if he had crossed the threshold or taken a step into a new place, a new atmosphere.

Stanzer locked up his office and led Ethan down three blocks and over several streets, to a long, dead-end street that overlooked the park.

Ethan passed an overgrown clump of bushes sitting on the corner and saw the house at the end of the street. He felt like he'd been slapped across the face with a length of the old-fashioned slate sidewalk under his feet. Gold and olive, with Victorian gingerbread and a wrap-around porch. Four stories tall. The sign in front of the wrought-iron fence read "Divine's Emporium."

All the dreams he had tried to forget, to push back into the neat closet in his mind where he put fever dreams and useless bits of trivia, came rushing out to his conscious mind. He stumbled a step from the physical shock, the pressure of it all pushing him along. For a few seconds his feet sped up their pace, but he regained control and walked beside Stanzer in the warm, bright afternoon.

Cautiously, Ethan tugged the sketch from his pocket and opened it. Nothing had changed. Why he expected some change in the sketch, he couldn't quite explain. Staring at the pencil lines, his imagination colored the hair gold and red, filled the eyes with blue like the sea, put roses in her cheeks and a curve to her lips, and colored them the shade of fresh raspberries.

"Dreams don't come true," he muttered as they passed through the wrought iron gate and approached the front porch.

"If you believe that," Stanzer said with a dry chuckle, "you're in the wrong place. Finding lost dreams and making them live is Angela's specialty."

"Is it?" Ethan jammed the sketch into his pocket.

His fingers curled around the talisman. How, when he hadn't put it in his pocket? An electric jolt shot through him and he nearly leaped up the sidewalk, onto the steps of the porch. Stanzer was right behind him. Ethan had time to wonder if the other P.I. was packing his gun, then his hand closed on the antique brass latch and he pushed the door open. He pulled his hand from his pocket and sternly ordered himself not to give Angela--or Annabelle, or whatever her name really was--the talisman until he had asked a lot of questions. The first of them being why she would appear here in the dead zone of information the Von Helados had given him.

Did they want him to find Annabelle or not? And if they did, why didn't they have any information, any clues or leads, pointing at Neighborlee, Ohio, and Divine's Emporium? Were they avoiding the town, or ...

A crazy thought came to him. Maybe they couldn't find the town, and they needed him to lead them there?

Delicate bells chimed over the door as he stepped into the shop. An image filled his head of a garden and sparkling, rainbow-hued creatures that flew about.

"Welcome to Divine's." The woman had a voice like the lower notes of a harp. The image of the garden faded from his mind as he turned around, looking at the shelves crowded with a bit of everything. He followed the voice to a large room with a counter and cash register and old-fashioned jars of candy lining the wall behind them. "Is there something in particular you're--"

She came into view, standing behind the counter. Their gazes met. Her face went white at the same moment the words died on her lips.

"Angela?" Stanzer stepped forward, putting himself between her and Ethan.

"It's all right. I just didn't expect this...so soon." Angela shook her head and stared into Ethan's eyes.

He could have sworn she spoke silently to him, and he didn't have the slightest idea what she said or how to answer. After a few thundering heartbeats that threatened to deafen him, she shook her head. A sad little smile curved her lips and only made the pallor of her face more pronounced.

"Need help?" Stanzer tugged aside his coat. Ethan couldn't see the holster, but he was sure now the other P.I. had brought his gun. They did take care of their own in Neighborlee, didn't they?

"It's all right. Let me deal with this on my own, will you?"

"Angela--"

"Please, Stayn, you don't want to get involved in this." She tried to smile. "You and Dawn have enough to handle, with the other children on their way."

"They're on their way? What did you--" Stanzer shook his head. "I ought to know by now not to question where you get your information. Are they all right?"

She glanced back at Ethan before she turned to Stanzer. "I only know they're ready to make their break for freedom. Be ready when they make contact again."

Ethan was both amused and pained to realize he made her nervous, afraid. A place inside him that he'd thought was permanently dead and numb now throbbed to aching life. Sorrow and fury choked him. She should never be afraid of anything. It was his job to defend her.

Where did that totally insane thought come from? He didn't know her. Dreams didn't come true. They had never met. She was a figment of his imagination. Correction: she looked like, sounded like, a figment of his imagination. Nothing more. Nothing connected them.

"You sure you're okay?" Stanzer said, when she gestured for him to go. "Angela, if this guy is trouble--"

"I'll explain later. Please, for the sake of the Hunt, leave." Resolve hardened her voice. Whatever weakness Ethan had seen in her a moment ago, it was gone.

Stanzer must have seen that. He gave Ethan one hard stare of warning and stomped down the hall to the front door. The chimes were silent, which somehow didn't surprise Ethan at all. Something about Divine's Emporium struck chords of recognition and warned him that whatever happened, he shouldn't be surprised.

"So, they call you Angela now?" The sooner he got this job started, the sooner it would be done, and the sooner he could leave. Ethan swore he heard soft voices whispering and giggling, but there was no one in the shop crowded with odd, glittering things. No one but him and Angela.

A sparkle in the air flew tight loops around his head and then zoomed down to settle on Angela's shoulder. Ethan could have sworn he heard a voice. A familiar, male voice, which made no sense. The words were indistinguishable. His ears buzzed and there was a momentary ache, as if he strained to hear something that wasn't there. He concentrated hard, erasing the light and sound from his consciousness, just as he banished the multi-colored, whispering, laughing lights that sometimes plagued him when he was tired and lonely, on the verge of sleeping or waking.

"Who sent you, and what did they tell you? What do they want this time? Who is it this time?" She had regained her color. Ethan wondered how Stanzer connected her with the sketch. There was only a ghost of a resemblance.

"Annabelle--" He pulled the sketch out of his pocket and smoothed it flat on the counter.

"Burn it. Please." Her voice cracked and she took a step back.

Ethan's jaw dropped. Color drained from her with every heartbeat; skin, hair, clothes, eyes. Another moment, would she become like the sketch?

He didn't care how impossible it was, Ethan picked up the sketch and tore it down the middle.

He *tried* to.

The paper wouldn't tear.

The color continued to drain from Angela's features.

"I don't have a match!"

She went to her knees, clutching at the counter, and gestured with a shaking hand. Ethan turned and saw a stained-glass oil lamp, sitting on a display shelf by the door. It hadn't been lit when he walked in. The flame wavered as if in a high wind, but nothing stirred inside the shop. He leaped down the aisle, yanked the chimney off the lamp and thrust the paper into the flame. The hot glass scorched his fingers. He dropped the chimney, but it didn't shatter when it hit the wooden floor. The paper vanished with a sigh and a puff of sour smoke. The flame grew stronger, and a sweet, fresh, citrus scent swept through the shop.

"Thank you." Angela pulled herself to her feet. She managed a wobbly smile and wiped beads of sweat off her forehead. A rough chuckle escaped her when Ethan staggered back toward the counter. "You don't believe in magic, do you?"

"I don't know what I believe."

"Do you at least believe the people who sent you to find me and gave you that sketch to use against me aren't my friends?"

He did believe, and it angered him to be used to hurt an innocent party. "Who are they, and what do they want?"

"I'm not sure *who* they are, though I have ideas. It should be obvious they want power over me." She caught her breath, looked away, then met his gaze again. "Can you tell me ... have we met before?"

He shrugged, to fight the shiver that filled him. At her words, the certainty swept over him that he did know her, and the shop felt familiar. Could he blame that on his dreams?

"Usually, I'm not at a loss. Usually, I know all the little secrets." She tried to laugh. "Now I know how everyone else feels when they come in here. It isn't pleasant, is it?"

"Depends on how much you have to be in control."

"We are all puppets in someone else's hands, one way or another. Control is a temporary gift, a responsibility more than a privilege." She rubbed her face with her fingertips, and it seemed to him she rubbed color back into her features, rolling away wrinkles.

That spark grew brighter, bigger on her shoulder. Ethan could have sworn he saw a person in the middle of the spark. He shook his head and looked away. A soft gasping laugh escaped Angela. When he looked back, the spark was gone.

"So... Angela, right?" He took a deep breath, consciously shoved away the tension tightening his gut again, and braced his arms on the counter directly opposite her. "I don't like it when people play games with me."

"Believe me, I am as much in the dark as you."

"Oh, I believe it." He yanked his gaze free of hers when he sensed something stirring inside him, reaching for a memory that stung and burned and flared bright enough to blind him. "I may not understand what just happened--"

"You don't believe because you don't want to believe."

"What does believing have to do with understanding?"

"Everything. But I think..." She took a step back from the counter, arms crossed, almost hugging herself, and tipped her head to one side as she studied him. "I think, for a time, your refusal to believe might be our armor and shield."

"Armor, huh?" He forced a brief chuckle to fight down the ache that shot through him at the word. "I'm no white knight, lady. Never have been, and after the things I've seen and done ... It'd take a miracle to make me one."

"Divine's Emporium specializes in miracles." That tightness around her eyes relaxed a little.

"Not doing you much good right now, is it?"

"The world fights against miracles, don't you know that? The world wants everything to be in neat, orderly, standard packages. Everything explainable and controllable and uniform. No one different from anyone else. Predictable. But that leads to such a plain, flat, monotone world."

She sighed and reached into a candy jar, pulled out something, and tossed it to him. "Where would we be without color and oddness and things that don't quite fit, to make us wake up?"

Ethan caught it, feeling sharp angles and a hard length in his palm before he opened his fingers and saw the rock candy stick lying in his palm. The crystals clung to a thin, pale blond wooden stick. They were multiple colors, some shimmering with a pearly gleam, others almost metallic.

"How did you--" He shook his head. Asking how someone made candy was a time waster. Unless of course the candy was laced with drugs or poison, and his gut instinct said Angela was the last person to stoop to such crude tactics. If she believed in magic as strongly as she seemed, she wouldn't need drugs to make the world beautiful and full of wonder. "I don't usually eat candy."

"You should. Children know how to enjoy small tastes and let treats be treats. It's when the world presses in on us and we think nothing can be wonderful that we start to be gluttons and greedy, and we want treats to be meals instead of high points." She tipped her head to one side and her smile softly grew, with a hint of mischief sparkling in those big eyes like the sea, daring him.

Growling so softly he only felt it in his throat, Ethan lifted the rock candy stick to his mouth and took a tentative lick.

He should have expected there to be more than just sweetness. More than just colored sugar crystallized on a stick. What he tasted, he wasn't quite sure. Could he taste memories? This was what the feeling and scent of the air after a raging thunderstorm would taste like, if that taste could be collected and condensed.

Ethan shook his head free of that fancy and lowered the stick. He could have sworn Angela blinked away a single tear when he didn't take a second lick. But that made no sense.

"Look--what I was going to say before--I don't know what's going on, but it's clear to me these people looking for you are up to no good. You're not their demented niece who ran away after a fire and thinks everyone in your family is dead, are you?"

"I have been in this town so long...if I ever had any family, they are long dead or have forgotten me. No, these people claiming to be my family are lying." She shook her head, her face going somber again, tightening around the eyes and mouth. "People lie for a reason. What do they hope to gain by lying about me?"

"That's what we need to find out."

"We?" That sparkle returned to her eyes.

It made him feel like he had taken a big whiff of oxygen, opened up something inside his head, let light in.

"Why 'we,' Mr. ..." She laughed. "I don't know your name."

"Ethan Jarrod." He held out his hand to shake hers without thinking. A cool feeling like dew and the breeze at dawn rushed over him when her long-fingered, smooth hand rested in his grasp. It took all his discipline to let go after that brief clasp and not hold on. Maybe yank her across the counter and into his arms.

The talisman in his pocket stung and burned through the cloth of his pants, and he flinched and tugged free.

"Ethan. Nice to... Well, not exactly nice to meet you. Strange. Disrupting. But I think I shall be glad we met. If only because I now have some warning about my enemies." Angela nodded and took a deep breath. "As I started to say, why do you say 'we,' Ethan?"

"I don't much like it when people try to use me to hurt other people. Turning people into tools, that's wrong. Lying to me, that makes me mad. Hurting you the way they did with that picture."

"But you don't quite believe in what happened there, do you?"

"Doesn't matter if I believe or not, I know what I saw. Something happened and it wasn't right. So, from where I'm standing, I owe these folks some payback. For me, if not for you. And I owe you something because I did hurt you, even if I didn't mean it."

"Which means you owe them even more, for using you that way." Her smile widened just a little, with a touch of weariness that made him want to sweep her up in his arms and carry her to some place quiet and shadowed and cool, so she could rest.

Ethan didn't quite understand that. He shook away the impulse like he pushed away the sense of those colored, laughing, whispering lights gathering around. That irritating spark had returned, sitting on the edge of the cash register, with a man's grinning face staring up at him from the center of the brightness.

"I'll be in touch--through Stanzer, okay?" He jammed his hand into his pocket and flinched when his fingers touched the talisman again. He yanked his hand out of his pocket, and for a second the talisman tried to stick to his fingers.

Ethan backed away from the counter, trying not to shake his hand to get rid of the sting from that contact. He needed to get some hand sanitizer, at the very least. He thought he had left the talisman in his desk back in his office. "We'll figure this out."

"I'm sure we will." She sighed and leaned forward, resting her elbows on the counter, and watched him step toward the doorway. "But will you enjoy the answers, Ethan?"

"Doesn't matter if we enjoy it or not. The truth is what's important." He paused, and for a moment teetered on the edge of letting her big eyes draw him back to the counter, to lean in close and stare into their jeweled depths. And do what, he wasn't quite certain. "Take care of yourself, Miss Angela."

"You too, Ethan."

He took a deep breath and held it until he was out the front door of Divine's Emporium, then let it out quickly and loudly.

"Spill," Stanzer said, before Ethan was off the porch and heading for the wrought iron gate. He stayed where he had probably been the entire time, leaning against a tree by the curb.

Ethan didn't hold anything back. After all, this was Stanzer's territory. He cared about Angela. If anyone had a clue how those stolen books and the Von Helados and Angela all tied together-- heck, how the laughing lights and other strange sounds and shadows and feelings tied in, too--he would. It took the entire walk back to Stanzer's office to relate the story and most of what he and Angela had said to each other.

"Trouble," Stanzer said, the first sound he had made since Ethan started his story.

When they walked into the office and he saw the young woman sitting at the computer, a shot of hungry envy socked him in the gut. It would be nice to have a partner, someone to work with. Someone to smile at him when he walked through the door like this girl looked at Stanzer.

"Big news," the girl said. She glanced at Ethan, and then tipped her head toward the screen, silently asking Stanzer what to do.

"Later. Angela's problem just got bigger."

Ethan flinched when a big spark just like the one that had been sitting on Angela's shoulder flew into the office. He tried not to watch as it flew circles around the girl, whom Stanzer introduced as Dawn, before it settled on his shoulder. That hint of a voice was stronger now. His head ached, temples and at the base of his neck. Ethan decided it might be wise to sit down before he fell like a toppled oak and cleared off Stanzer's desk.

"You okay?" Stanzer settled on the edge of the desk, frowning down at him. Dawn ran to a mini-fridge and pulled out a bottle of water to give to him.

"Guess I've been pulling too many all-nighters in a row," Ethan offered. He nodded his thanks as he took the bottle. He limited himself to small sips as he talked. "That sketch must have had some drug on it--bad smell when it burned." He felt better just speaking that theory. It was a better explanation than the others that pressed at his conscious thoughts, which he refused to consider. Not now anyway, in the light of day.

"Later," Stanzer said, looking at Dawn.

Ethan decided he really hated them for that instant communication in just a glance, a frown, a flick of the eyes.

That spark flared brighter. Stanzer seemed to be looking at it and nodding. He focused on Ethan again, with an assessing, weighing look that was all too familiar. Ethan had seen his reflection wear that expression when he studied people he wasn't sure he could trust. Part of him rose up in protest. Hadn't he been as honest as he could be with these people? They were the ones with secrets, hidden knowledge they weren't sharing with him. They were the ones with strange enemies. They were the ones who believed in magic and dreams and lived in a town that reeked with otherness.

"What's Lanie's schedule, do you know?" Stanzer slid off the desk and looked over his shoulder at Dawn.

"Full day today." She settled down at her desk again. "Truth or consequences?"

"Let's hope not." He gestured for Ethan. "You up for walking?"

"I'm fine." Ethan stood, more relieved than he liked to admit when the room didn't spin around him. He gestured thanks to Dawn and put down the half-empty bottle of water on the desk. He didn't ask where they were going until they had put two intersections between them and Stanzer's office.

"I have someone I want you to meet. Or maybe the better way to say it is, I want her to meet you." Stanzer stuck his hands in his pockets and sauntered down the street as if they weren't doing anything other than enjoying the clear, bright, warm weather.

They walked in silence, crossing several intersections. Stanzer was one of those comfortable people who didn't feel the need to fill the quiet with talk. Ethan appreciated that. After they made a right turn, the other P.I. gestured at the building ahead of them.

The sprawling building looked like several separate buildings had been connected together. The sign in front proclaimed it the *Neighborlee Tattler*. Ethan supposed that made sense. Newspaper reporters and private investigators made good partners. He wondered what Stanzer thought he could tell this reporter. Then he considered the way the other man had rephrased it--he wanted her to meet Ethan.

Before they had crossed the parking lot that stretched in front of the building, the door opened and a woman in a wheelchair rolled out and down the short ramp. She had tangled, dark hair, and wore capris, sandals, and a tie-dyed T-shirt that seemed to swirl inward as she pumped her wheels, crossing to meet them.

"Hey, Stanzer. Maurice said you had a new friend you wanted me to meet." She tipped her head to one side, looking up at Ethan. A frown dug around her eyes and flattened her mouth as Stanzer introduced her as Lanie Zephyr, copy editor and columnist.

"Something wrong?" Ethan had to ask.

"Just wondering... You aren't into dragon-slaying, are you?"

He backed up a step, startled at her words, and feeling as if the parking lot had tried to slide out from under his feet like a slippery rug on slick-polished marble.

She snorted. "Sorry. I just get these impressions of people when I first meet them, sometimes. Ask anybody around here, they'll tell you it's leftover brain damage from when I ended up in this thing." She slapped one of her wheels. "So, what's up?"

"Ethan, just trust me on this, okay?" Stanzer gestured at Lanie. "I want you to hold Lanie's hand and tell her everything that happened when you went to see Angela."

"Hold her hand?" For about two seconds, Ethan seriously considered just turning and walking away. His weirdness quotient for the next several months had been used up in just one day in Neighborlee.

"I'm a reporter. I'm good at reading people," Lanie said, holding out her hand. "Stanzer wants to get my impression of your reactions, that's all. Any movements you make, if you start to sweat, that sort of thing. Intensifies if we're touching."

Ethan didn't buy that explanation for one minute, but his gut instinct was working overtime in this town. When logic didn't help, he knew better than to ignore that silent, often inexplicable guide. He wiped his hand on his thigh and gave it into Lanie's grip. He flinched a little, feeling the strength, the calluses, in that lean hand. Then he thought about the encounter with Angela and decided to start the story with getting the job from the Von Helados.

He left out the talisman and the report on the discoloration coating it. He told her about the empty circle on the map when he noted all the locations of the leads the Von Helados had given him, and Neighborlee in the center of the empty circle. He described the sketch, Stanzer taking him to Divine's, and Angela's reaction to the sketch. He included the agreement he had made with Angela, because he sensed trying to keep it a secret would be useless. She would tell her friends and withholding that bit of information might work against him.

He decided his strongest emotion was jealousy. He wished he had people to gather around him when there was a threat, like the support Angela had in this town. Ethan usually enjoyed his solitude, his lack of encumbrances, freedom to move, and no one to be used against him when he angered people. Not now. For the first time in what felt like decades, he felt alone, abandoned, maybe even cast out. It hurt.

"You don't want to believe in what happened," Lanie said, after she let go of his hand. She sat back in her wheelchair, eyes narrowed, looking up at him. "But you're one of those logical guys who's so honest, it hurts. You won't throw aside what you saw until you get proof it wasn't real." She snorted. "But there are a ton of things you saw that you didn't want to see."

"Yeah, and that makes sense?" Ethan wanted to laugh. It caught in his throat. He thought of the laughing, colored lights, and that spark that seemed to talk and have a man's face.

"You're on the up-and-up as much as you can be. Everything that happened freaks you, just a little. And you've got some knight in shining armor tendencies." Her face softened a little. "You're pissed at these Von Helados. Did you know *helado* in Spanish means *ice*? Or was that *ice cream*? Anyway, Von hints at maybe

Dutch or German or something, so I don't know what the connection is, but... You're planning on pretending to keep working with these creeps until you figure out what they really want from Angela, aren't you?"

"Yeah, that's pretty much the plan."

"You're okay, Ethan Jarrod. You need to get those blinders off your eyes, and you need to figure out a bunch of things, to let go and enjoy the unbelievable and just plain freaky, but you're okay."

"Okay?" He frowned at Stanzer, who visibly relaxed about ten degrees. "You brought me here to get a second opinion on whether I could be trusted, is that it? What does she do? Read auras? Read minds?"

Ethan caught himself just before he wiped the hand Lanie had held on the leg of his pants for a second time. "Okay, maybe it's the heat. Maybe it's -- I don't know what it is. I have to get out of here before my head explodes. No offense."

"I'd be worried if you weren't hacked off," Lanie said.

For a second, Ethan choked on something that could have been a growl or a burst of laughter. Exhaustion wiped away the fury that had been trying to coil up from inside him.

"I'll be in touch, Stanzer."

The two men shook hands, and Ethan nodded to Lanie before turning and heading down the street. He was pretty sure how to get to the bed & breakfast from here. He needed to be alone.

<div style="text-align: center">~~~~~</div>

"What's the scoop?" Maurice climbed out from the tangle of Lanie's hair, where he had been hiding. He felt a flicker of sympathy for Ethan, realizing the P.I. could partly see and hear him, and guessing how uncomfortable it made him.

"He's pretty much telling the truth," Lanie said.

"Pretty much?" Stanzer turned, looking down the street where Ethan's tall figure strode away with a stiff-legged gait.

"He's not lying, but there are things he senses aren't true and he's avoiding them. I have never read anybody like him before." She wiped her hand on her T-shirt. "That guy has a lot of problems he doesn't even know about. Makes everything murky. Of course, my human lie detector gig isn't always reliable, so who knows?"

"You mentioned something about slaying dragons before you touched him," Maurice said.

"Yeah. Just when you guys were coming across the parking lot, I had a glimpse of him in armor, rushing into something that sure seemed like flames, holding out his shield and waving this killer sword that would make Conan jealous. I've never seen anybody so pissed and scared at the same time." She rubbed her eyes and let out a groan. "Times like these make me sure God has a really nasty sense of humor. I never understand these visions until after the explanations all fall together, but I know I'm getting clues that could help if I could just figure them out."

"Maybe since this seems to revolve around Angela, you should tell her what you saw?" Stanzer suggested.

"What makes you think she doesn't know all this already?"

"Yeah," Maurice said. "She always knows things and keeps them to herself until the right time. The thing is..." He shuddered a little, feeling a wave of nausea from worry mixed with fear. His wings fluttered like a storm-strength gale had just gone through.

"Usually she tells you, if nobody else?" Lanie guessed. "And if she hasn't shared anything with you, then maybe she's having a hard time figuring things out?"

"If she's lost," Stanzer said, as his face hardened with resolve, "it'll help her to know what the rest of us are picking up on. Or just knowing we're in this with her."

Chapter Seven

Tears threatened Angela's self-control when Lanie, Maurice, and Stanzer laid out what they had seen, their impressions of Ethan, and their theories. She fought them for a few heartbeats but realized that was ridiculous. She was only hurting herself. These were her friends, her family. If she couldn't be weak and weep in front of them, she was entirely alone in the universe.

Giving herself permission to let go and cry, naturally, dried up the aching, weary feeling. A few tears trickled down along her nose, but there were no sobs or shaking. She hugged Lanie and Stanzer and made them all laugh when she threatened to save up a big hug for Maurice when he was full-size again.

"I have been having strange dreams of a knight," she admitted. Her throat ached faintly with the effort of forming those words. "There is an overgrown garden that I sense was once a sanctuary, a paradise. It is dark, and the darkness is cold, and on the far side of a patch of moonlight I see him. At first I don't realize he is there, just a shape, perhaps a tree or a stone pillar, it varies from dream to dream. But when I see him and I realize he is a man, he frightens me. And he is angry. So furiously angry."

"Why?" Maurice asked.

"If I knew that, the dream wouldn't be so disturbing. I could do something about it." She sighed and looked around the sun-soaked backyard of her house.

Angela hadn't let herself indulge in relaxing in her garden in the warmth and sunshine since that night when she had been attacked. She still wasn't convinced the theft of the books and Ethan's appearance with that sketch that had tried to drain the life from her were related. Chances were very good that one had merely opened her up to the other. Perhaps the resonance from the attack had alerted other enemies to the presence of Divine's, or even to her existence, and let them know she was weakened.

"Stayn?" Dawn came around the side of the house, nearly glowing in her excitement. "Sorry." She stopped short, reacting to the somberness of the group.

"No, it's all right." Angela gestured for the girl to come join them, on the benches and around her swing. "John said you had contact with more members of the Hunt. Good news?"

"They're on their way. Fleeing major trouble." She swallowed hard, losing the glow for a moment. Angela ached for Dawn, for the disparity in time that kept her and Stanzer from complete partnership that would strengthen both of them.

Time works against us all, she mused, *perhaps the most potent weapon in our enemies' hands.*

Dawn quickly told them about four other refugees from their homeworld. They had been gathered together under false pretenses by a rich, powerful, cruel man who knew far too much about them. He had the power and influence to falsify records and make threats if the young people he claimed were his long lost, kidnapped grandchildren, weren't given into his custody.

He had experimented on them, under the pretense of trying to awaken their memories, and instead had awakened their talents long before the proper time. The four had realized that this rich old man, Wolcott, was actually one of them, a traitor who had come with the Hunt to Earth, planning all along to betray them into Gahlmorag's hands. The disparity in time and place had kept this man separate from the rest of the Hunt, and allowed him to grow up and grow old, and powerful. He had killed his own son when his heir chose to be loyal to the Hunt.

"The thing is, Cinden says living here too long will eventually make us just as sick as Wolcott is now." Dawn glanced down at a printout of the communication that had come through the website she had designed to make contact with other members of the Hunt. "And while we can breed with the people of Earth, it's not a good idea. Oberon, Wolcott's grandson, had some major genetic drift and damage that was killing him, maybe even faster than Wolcott."

She swallowed hard and locked gazes with Stanzer. "The Lai family comes from very strong healers. Cinden's awakened gift let her cleanse and heal a lot of things, straighten out what had been twisted. Obie has sworn to the Hunt, and he's run away with them. They're heading our way, but Cinden is afraid there's going to be a showdown, eventually. Wolcott knows what to look for, and how to identify members of the Hunt. Now that he knows about the time disparity, he'll find us. If he hasn't found us already."

"Let him," Angela said. "Bring the others here. If need be, we'll send all of you through a dimensional slit to hide, but your enemy will only grow stronger the longer you run and hide. Better to face him now, while he's still smarting from the loss of his grandson."

"But if a delay lets him get stronger, won't it let us grow stronger?" Dawn asked.

"Not if we spend all our time hiding and trying to ward off attack." Stanzer shook his head. "We need to go on the offensive as soon as possible. Angela, I hate to ask this of you, in the middle of all the trouble you're facing--"

"Ethan understands, and he's not going to cooperate with the Von Helados." Gratified by the concern of her friends, a pleasant warmth stole through Angela, pushing away some of the cold and tension. She wasn't alone. That bit of knowledge was more important than anything. "Divine's Emporium exists to help and to heal and to provide sanctuary. Bring your friends here. We have a reprieve. Perhaps Ethan is such a strong disbeliever, he'll not only withstand anything else these people try to do, but he will convince them that I don't exist."

She held onto her serene smile and managed not to shudder as she relived, just for a moment, the draining feeling that washed over her, sucking at her energy, her mind, her soul, the very colors of her life, when Ethan had pulled out that pencil sketch. If he hadn't succeeded in destroying it, if Maurice hadn't shouted "Fire!" and lit the first lantern he could find, that sketch might very well have drained all her color and life, leaving her little more than a pencil sketch. Like a reverse portrait of Dorian Gray situation.

The farther Ethan Jarrod stayed away from Divine's, from Neighborlee, and from her, the happier Angela would be.

Which was sadly, bitterly ironic, because for a few moments there, among all the chaos and terror of her encounter with the man, Angela had the strangest urge to beg him to stay with her. Something in her insisted, for just a few heartbeats, that they had promised eternity to each other.

But how could that be when she was sure, just a heartbeat later, that she didn't know him? How could she, when he clearly did not believe in otherness, in magic, in all the things she had devoted her life to guarding?

She turned the focus of her thoughts and energies to helping Dawn and Stanzer and their fellow refugees. That was the purpose of her existence, after all: to protect the innocent and defenseless, to confuse and frustrate and confound the arrogant and powerful and cruel, and to nourish the magical and rare and unique.

~~~~~

Ethan dreamed five nights in a row of Angela and Divine's Emporium. Yet he couldn't be sure she was the same magical lady of his previous dreams, and the shop was the same house. Something had changed. He saw her and the house from a distance. A haze of light acted as a barrier, keeping him from stepping out of the darkness and crossing the street, or climbing the hill from the forest and approaching the house. When he let himself think about his dreams, he suspected that if he could push the wrought iron gate open and step into the light surrounding the house, he would have answers. All the answers he could ever want.

Each morning, he woke from his dreams feeling cold and dusty inside, and more tired than he had felt when he went to sleep. Each night, the distance between him and Divine's Emporium lengthened, until on the last night he had only a glimpse of movement through the windows, and could only assume that was Angela, moving about safe within the walls of her house, where there was light and music and warmth.

The sixth morning, he woke rested, yet with an ache inside. After almost an entire day of infrequently gnawing on the question of what could be wrong, he realized he had not dreamed at all.

That was a good thing, wasn't it?

He busied himself investigating the second batch of leads the Von Helados had given him, and then following up on more they sent him just after he returned from his trip to Neighborlee. It worried Ethan that these new clues were all inside the empty circle that surrounded the town, creating a new, smaller circle of empty space. He felt like he had while watching his first motion picture, knowing what danger lay around the corner for the hapless heroine, listening to the other people in the audience calling out warnings, and knowing it was useless.

For a moment, he gnawed on the oddness of that memory. Film audiences were too sophisticated to do that, so why did he distinctly remember that happening? And why was the heroine
~~~~~

tied to the railroad tracks in his memory? Nobody did that to heroines in movies nowadays. Mostly because heroines knew how to kick the snot out of villains who resorted to such tactics. A villain who would use a Taser or other technology to get the drop on the heroine wouldn't resort to killing her with a train. Besides, trains had too much safety gear to let something like that happen.

What was he doing, gnawing on a memory like that, nit-picking the rationale of movie plots? Ethan worried that something was definitely wrong with him, that he let himself get sidetracked with such illogical concerns. Maybe when that book thief Tasered him, it had scrambled the wrong circuits and he was still recovering? Could he get brain damage from a Taser?

He had to get back to work. What had he been thinking about? Oh yeah--the smaller circle of emptiness, with Neighborlee almost dead center. Ethan picked up the phone twice to call Stanzer and give him warning, but after a few seconds of thought, put down the phone again. As long as that empty circle, thirty miles in diameter, lay around Neighborlee like a buffer zone, the town and Divine's Emporium and Angela were safe. Maybe something was keeping the Von Helados from approaching her. Then again, the new batch of clues certainly seemed to indicate they *were* getting closer, as if they were wearing down the barrier or whoever blocked them.

Neither theory made any sense. He snarled at himself for getting off track again and refocused on the task at hand.

A search program he set up gleaned any mention from the Internet and law enforcement sources about unusual activity around the town. Just in case. He also did some reverse investigation of the Von Helados, to try to keep track of their actions. He wouldn't put it past them to have him do the preliminary work of proving all the other possible Annabelles weren't legitimate. Then to keep from paying him the final lump sum fee, due when he turned her over to them, they would swoop in, snatch up Angela, and drag her off to the dark, dreary mausoleum mansion they lived in.

He nearly laughed when he decided he wouldn't turn anyone over to those people just for the sake of money. Even if Angela was Annabelle, he wouldn't turn her over to her relatives. If they were her relatives. There was no proof. Maybe that was what he should be working on: not proving they were her relatives, but proving they weren't related to Angela in any way.

Just because Angela looked something like Annabelle, if there had ever been a real Annabelle, that didn't mean he would allow the Von Helados to take her. Just in that brief, strange, unbalancing encounter, Ethan had learned enough to know Angela belonged in Divine's Emporium. They were part of each other, as if she and the house had grown together on that spot, like two intertwined trees.

Making the resolution gave him more peace than he had known in a long time. He felt a touch of amusement to realize he hadn't even noticed he *didn't* have peace until then. He wasn't quite ready to give up the hard-won stability of his life and the logic and reason that guided his steps. Yet at the same time, he liked this sense that stepping out in faith, against logic, had caused something to slip back into place in his mind and heart, and soul. If he even had a soul.

The night, he dreamed again of standing a few steps away from the porch of Divine's Emporium at night. Angela stood on the porch, in the familiar blue dress. She was surrounded by streamers of light in multiple colors, like gossamer scarves stirred by a swirling wind. She held out her hand, beckoning to him to come up, into the light. Something pushed him and he stumbled forward, his legs stiff-locked with fear and cold. A deep-seated fury churned inside him, eating away at him with icy flames. Angela caught hold of his hand and managed to pull him close enough to the porch that his foot banged against the bottom step.

She spoke, but he couldn't hear her voice. He knew she was begging him to step up. She could only hold his hand and pull, but she couldn't bring him up onto the porch unless he took the first step. He wanted to take that step. His legs stayed stiff. All he could do was tighten his grip on her hand, until he thought he would crush the fragile bones. But she didn't cry out in pain, didn't react except to smile and pull harder and keep begging him, silently, to step up.

Something grabbed him, pulling him backward. Pulling Angela off the porch with him. He tried to let go of her hand. He couldn't move his fingers. She screamed. The sound shattered the throbbing silence and threatened to turn his bones to dust. Still, he couldn't move, couldn't let go of her. He sank backward, swallowed up by the darkness.

A faint glow surrounded Angela's hand as it was pulled into darkness with him. Ethan watched, horrified, as that glow turned to a pale, gray, writhing luminescence like rotting stumps in a swamp. Her soft, slim hand shriveled and turned to bones, and the shriveling traveled up her arm. Angela struggled, holding onto the porch railing with one hand, not even able to scream now, and the terror in her eyes slashed at his soul.

With a roar of fury and a feeling of blood gushing up from deep inside him, filling his lungs and throat, Ethan opened his hand. He felt as if his bones were shattering to dust, but he managed to let go of her. She fell back against the wall of Divine's, cradling her shriveled, gray arm, and wept as he tumbled backward and fell down into the darkness.

He woke with a shout, rolled out of his bed, and struck his head against the nightstand. He huddled on the floor, gasping for breath, welcoming the feeling of hot blood streaming down his sweating face and the pain that told him this was no dream.

That settled it. He was never going near Neighborlee, Ohio, or Divine's Emporium, ever again. Not if there was a chance he could be part of killing Angela.

~~~~~

Angela found great satisfaction in helping the five refugee children who showed up in Neighborlee after weeks of anticipation and stealthy travel. When she heard all the details of what Wolcott had done in his quest to control members of the Hunt, she wanted him humiliated as well as frustrated and defeated. She busied herself settling and equipping the five fugitives: Cinden, Sereena, Rob, and Dale, and their new recruit, Obie, Wolcott's grandson. She was especially pleased when Cinden saw Maurice the moment she stepped into Divine's Emporium.

Only a few days after their arrival, Wolcott's men came into Neighborlee. That confirmed Dawn and Cinden's fear. Wolcott had known about Dawn and Stanzer all along but had held back because he couldn't yet twist records to falsify authority over them and couldn't intimidate people into giving him what he wanted.

When the first uneasy ripples of reaction to the invasion moved through the foundation of the town, Angela couldn't at first discern the source. Did it come from Big Ugly, the enemy underground? Or did the defensive energy of Neighborlee react to the presence of the invaders? Despite appearances, did Wolcott and perhaps some of his minions have more otherworldly talent and power than the five fugitives had guessed? She scolded herself for being upset, feeling betrayed, that Wolcott's men were able to enter Neighborlee. The shield around their town, which had interfered with the last invasion attempt, hadn't failed them. It wasn't made to keep out
~~~~~

ordinary Humans, until they had been so thoroughly suborned by malevolent energies they became infected with the same evil, even if subconsciously. Just as the P.I. Simon Jones had been, back in February. Wolcott's men were still ordinary Humans, even if they were evil. If Wolcott could be repelled by the shield remained to be seen. He was a member of the Hunt, even if he had vowed falsely all those years ago when the Hounds brought him to Earth.

Occasionally, for a moment or two at a time, she wondered if the silence from Ethan Jarrod was because he had been thoroughly suborned by the Von Helados, whoever they were, whoever they served, and the shield around Neighborlee had kept him from returning. Angela knew better than to ask.

She said nothing about the sensation of uneasiness or her questions. The safety of the Hunt was her primary concern now. She wove options and plans together and waited for news of the strangers asking about five teen newcomers.

The fact that she couldn't discern immediately the source of the imbalance and disturbance worried her and showed her just how much she had let the events of the last few weeks affect her. Several times, she caught herself walking up the stairs to the second-floor landing, to stare at the spot in the wallpaper where she thought she caught glimpses of the stone gates of the hidden garden. She knew she hadn't imagined it, because Lanie had mentioned seeing the garden, years ago. That had been another perilous time when the enemy had struck and drained her to a frightening level.

One time, angry with herself, she brushed her fingertips over a section of the wallpaper where she thought the latch of the silver gate should be. Angela gasped, feeling the cool of the silver, the muted tingle of sleeping magic, seeping up through the paper.

"One way or another," she whispered, "this must come to an end."

She sent her consciousness deeper into the walls and foundation of the house, drawing on the seepage of magic from all the dimensional slits and doorways. When she went to bed that night, she called the winkies to her and asked to borrow their energy. They settled all over her and her bed, so her room glowed in a rich, deep purple luminescence that lulled her to sleep and helped her control her dreaming. All that night, she visited her acquaintances and allies, warning them of the battle she sensed coming. It comforted her and helped her find her balance again, to discuss what those on the other side would do to guard their doorways if anything happened to her, and the watchtower that was Divine's Emporium was compromised.

Lanie had drafted her Star Trek club to watch for strangers poking their noses where they didn't belong in town, strangers asking questions about the five teens staying with Dawn and Stanzer. She'd told them to take note of where the strangers went, who they talked to, and what they learned. Athena and Doni and their friends were on the alert. Gordon Priebe recruited friends in the Neighborlee police department to help. He had the support of Chief Tanner to simply watch and not react, and not cooperate with the strangers. The Longfellow family and the Zephyrs helped settle the five teens in the apartments Stanzer had prepared for members of the Hunt, and kept watch.

Angela found satisfaction in knowing the statement still held true: Neighborlee took care of its own. By the time Wolcott's men arrived to ask their questions, most of the residents of the town either knew of the refugee status of the five teens and had promised to help protect them, or they simply knew these hard-eyed strangers had invaded to cause trouble. Still, the showdown and confrontation came far too quickly for her tastes.

She didn't quite approve of the games the seven members of the Hunt played with Wolcott's men, the risks they ran leading them on a wild goose chase to the quarries. Despite their other-worldly origins and talents, they were still children. Stanzer was the only adult among them, with Dawn the next oldest at nearly eighteen. But she admired their bravado and their mature realization that the sooner they faced down their enemy and forced his hand, the safer they would be. Even though it made her uneasy to be away from Divine's Emporium at nightfall, she had to be there to support Dawn and Stanzer and their allies.

Wolcott accepted the Hunt's proposal: healing in exchange for leaving them entirely alone. Angela didn't believe for a moment he would live up to the agreement once he got what he wanted. Cinden's too-soon awakened powers, her ability to heal him of decades of damage from living in an alien world, made her a priceless commodity. Wolcott would want to control her, to sell her healing gift to the highest bidder, and eventually hand over to

Gahlmorag. The other members of the Hunt who had escaped Wolcott had also had their hereditary gifts forced awake, for his profit. It was too soon to tell if they had been damaged in any way by the acceleration.

Besides, there was one detail no one mentioned but was very obvious: the Hunt wanted to settle here in Neighborlee, where Dawn and Stanzer had prepared a home for them, a headquarters. They had to deal with Wolcott permanently, so he wouldn't spy on them or try to control them from a distance or eventually attempt to take them into custody. Until then, they wouldn't be safe, and neither would the secrets of the town be safe.

"Basically, we're depending on him being the liar and cheat and selfish brute he's proven himself to be all along," Stanzer said, when they discussed their options. "He's already forfeited the help and protection of the Hounds. When he breaks his vow and strikes at us, especially Cinden after she heals him... Well, we're hoping for a lot of fireworks, to put it mildly."

"Hey, I've seen your big puppy dogs in action," Maurice remarked, his voice and expression sour, but mischief in his eyes. "You hope this bozo steps in the doodoo up to his neck and really fries himself good."

"Yeah, that's a nice way of putting it." Stanzer's smile faded quickly.

Angela ached for him, seeing the weariness that shadowed his eyes and drew lines around his mouth. He was responsible for six minors, though Dawn would soon be a legal adult. Stanzer had to keep them safe, guide them in growing into their roles in the Hunt, and figure out what they would do to save their world whenever they managed to go home. Until they found more adult members of the Hunt, the pressure on him had to be incredible. She wasn't quite sure what to do to help him, other than to offer a sounding board and guidance, provide clothes and housing, and arrange for legal guardianship for the younger ones.

With all her senses doubly on the alert, she didn't need to be told by those standing sentinel duty at the major roads into town, when Wolcott's big black limousine and his musclemen in their cars crossed the border into Neighborlee. She was disappointed, but not surprised, when the shield didn't stop Wolcott from entering. The very air and ground shivered in revulsion at the presence of one who had broken sacred vows for the sake of power.

The sickness in Wolcott's body sent a stinging sensation through the air in waves, like ripples spreading out from a stone thrown into a still, shallow pond. The body reflected the soul. This soul was so diseased that nothing done by Cinden as a healer or Serena as a visionary and mind-healer would repair that damage. It had been done by choice, self-inflicted, and proudly embraced.

Angela stood at a distance in the park, where Cinden and the other members of the Hunt had set their meeting. She watched Wolcott's car park. The old, sick traitor climbed out and into a wheelchair, to be pushed up onto the stage of the natural amphitheater. Angela felt the shock waves go down into the ground. She caught her breath as the cold, hungry, sleeping awareness underneath Neighborlee stirred, awakening. She felt the dimensional walls shudder, felt the pressing of the enemy's strength and sentience, testing the barriers that kept it from entirely manifesting into this particular dimension.

Winkies gathered around her, thickening the air, responding to her call. They covered her in a cloak, loaning her their strength. She dug her bare feet into the grass, sending roots of awareness and her personal energy into the soil to reinforce that protective barrier. She flung her hands into the air and sent strength into the shield around her town and the parklands surrounding it.

"What was that?" Lanie whispered, wheeling up behind Angela.

"What was what?" She opened her eyes and sputtered a breathless laugh when she couldn't see for a moment, her vision clouded by pink and yellow and violet winkies.

"Like a big old bell rang, just once. A bell about the size of the whole town. I can still feel it, buzzing in my bones." She pointed at the ground. "Big Ugly isn't waking up again, is it?"

"No. Thank goodness."

"Yeah, one master villain at a time, please." Lanie turned to study the shimmering power that covered Cinden. She crossed the amphitheater stage as Wolcott's man helped him get out of the chair to lie on his back. "Too bad we're the good guys."

"Who says?" Maurice quipped, flying up to join them. He snapped off a salute and came in for a landing on Lanie's shoulder. "Why's it bad to be the good guys?"

"Now's the perfect opportunity for Cinden to off the creepazoid, while he's totally helpless." She glanced at them and snorted. "Did you ever watch that really corny Flash Gordon movie from the 80s, with Max von Sydow and Timothy Dalton?"

"Is that a hint to watch it, or a warning?"

"I think I know what scene you're referring to," Angela said, grateful for Lanie's insertion of humor into the tense moment.

"There's this scene where Dale, Flash's erstwhile girlfriend--" Lanie stuck her tongue out at Maurice when he snorted and muttered, "Erstwhile!" "She's up against Ming's daughter, whatever her name is. Space bimbo, all in leather. Anyway, she explains why Earth people can't do some nasty, vengeful thing that, when you really think about it, is totally logical and would save everybody a lot of trouble in the end. And she finishes up with, 'And that's why we're better than you are,' or something like that."

She sighed and slumped in her wheelchair. "And that's a good thing, I guess, because I would not want to be the one to tell a kid Cinden's age she needs to kill the nasty old codger while he's under her hands. Although, as a healer, she certainly has to know how to break the Human body to be able to fix it."

"Did you know the geezer actually tried to marry her, when they were kids back on the home planet?" Maurice offered.

"His family tried to arrange a marriage," Angela corrected. "He was only a few years older than her, at the time. And even back then, there were questions about the honor and loyalty of his clan."

"Even more reason for her to want to totally destroy the guy," Lanie said. Her cell phone went off, making her flinch and sit up straight again. She grinned when Angela sighed at the rollicking tune of *The Pirates Who Don't Do Anything*. Her grin faded quickly as she listened to her caller. She snapped off an affirmative and shut the phone. "Second wave moving in."

"Of course." Angela felt almost relieved to know the expected had happened. More of Wolcott's men had moved into position, surrounding the park, just as Stanzer had anticipated.

Villains were predictable. Promises never applied to them, unless it was to their advantage, and they always tried to stack the deck.

Chapter Eight

"Look out," Lanie muttered, as Wolcott sat up and jabbed something at Cinden. From the spark it gave off, it was probably a Taser.

The other members of the Hunt stepped out of hiding. Their voices carried, but not their words. Wolcott laughed, sneering at them, arguing. Thunder crackled through the air as the sky turned black like a heavy curtain slamming down, and a stiff wind that swirled down from everywhere at once blew through the park.

Hounds flashed into being, surrounding the amphitheater. Wolcott's men went flying, surrounded by silver sparks, or bowled over and knocked unconscious by the interdimensional guardian beasts. Wolcott got up and flung his weapon at Cinden as he turned to flee. A single Hound appeared from a slit in the air, making the Taser vanish in a flare of light. Then it knocked the man down and sat on him. It grew to a beast five times the size it had been.

And took Wolcott's head into its mouth.

The seven members of the Hunt clung together, looking away. Angela focused on the face of young Obie Wolcott, who had taken his grandfather's place, making good on the vows his ancestors had falsely made. She pitied the boy, seeing his grandfather's punishment. It had to be hard, knowing his grandfather had considered his father a weakling and a traitor, and had him killed.

The first shock wave of power rushing out from the Hounds reached Angela, Lanie and Maurice. Lanie snatched Maurice out of the air, clutching him close, while Angela bowed herself over Lanie's wheelchair and they clung together. The power didn't disturb the trees and grass, but the psionic equivalent of a heavy, grit-filled wind scorched the three of them. Angela's fingers and toes and nose tingled, and her hair stood on end for a few painful moments. A brilliant flash of lightning shot up from the ground where the Hound had crouched, slicing into the sky.

This time, Angela heard the single chiming of an enormous bell, deep and strong, ponderous in its reverberation. Just as Lanie had described it, the bell sounded as big as the town.

She shuddered, wondering who else might have heard that bell ring. The possibilities were endless, both good and bad. And so were the reactions.

~~~~~

Ethan struggled out of his desk chair, knocking his mug of coffee off the desk onto the floor. He rubbed his arms and chest, trying to relieve the sensation of ants and sand being rubbed into his skin, fighting the urge to tear off all his clothes and scratch.

As the *snap-rasp* of his mug shattering on the tile floor slapped at his ears, the itching sensation settled into his bones. Breathless, he leaned forward, bracing himself on his desk, head bowed. Through half-closed eyes, he caught a sudden, brief flare of light from a half-open drawer. Ethan snatched at the drawer pull, yanking it open.

The Von Helados' talisman rippled like it was underwater, and the glow faded to a dirty yellow luminescence before dying away completely. He stared at it for five minutes, just to make sure it wouldn't try anything else. Then he pulled out his handkerchief and folded it four times before using it to insulate his hand. He grasped the beaded chain and picked it up, holding it out so the talisman hung at eye-level.

He should have thrown it out or tried to give it back to the Von Helados after his last progress report, when the last leads had all proven useless. They had paid him for his time and provided no more clues or leads, and he had let them leave their working relationship open. That was a mistake, he knew now. It somehow left him in partnership with them, and his gut instinct insisted, loudly, that made him weak. Vulnerable. Manipulable.

"What did you think you were doing?" he scolded himself as he flung the talisman back into the dirty, cracked mug in his drawer where he had kept it. "Protecting her by making sure they couldn't use it against her? They probably have a dozen of these. Two dozen. And just as many P.I.s investigating different states, probably." Ethan rubbed his face with his open hands and sank back down into his chair.

He didn't like the sweat filming his face, any more than he liked the suspicion that he had felt an echo of something that had happened in Neighborlee. Logic said that was impossible, a
~~~~~

figment of his imagination. He was tired, maybe getting sick, having delusions.

So how come the longer he argued with himself, the more certain his gut became that he hadn't heard or seen the last of the Von Helados or Neighborlee, or Angela of Divine's Emporium?

Despite the chill down his spine and the throbbing in his temples, a smile curved one side of his mouth, in anticipation of seeing her golden hair, sea-blue eyes, and raspberry-colored lips again. Maybe if he found a way to be helpful, he would finally learn if they tasted as sweet as the real thing.

~~~~~

Late that night, Maurice shivered as the discord in the magic enveloping Divine's Emporium jolted him awake. Like everyone else, he was exhausted after cleaning up the mess with Wolcott. His brain felt fuzzy for a few seconds, even as the magic buzzed in his wings. A sense of urgency ignited him into action. He took a running leap, slamming open the doors of the cupboard holding his bedroom and wardrobe, inside Angela's apartment. He fell halfway to the floor before he got his wings untangled and swooped upward again. The swirling in the air tingled with Angela's presence. The discord wove through it. Even suspecting it was a waste of his time, Maurice flew into Angela's bedroom.

Her bed was empty.

Half-closing his eyes, he followed the trail in the air, out of her apartment, and nearly ran into Angela's back as she shuffled down the hall toward a silvery glowing spot in the wall opposite the landing. Swallowing a yelp, Maurice flew around and got in front of her. He wasn't surprised to see her eyes were closed. The sight of the tears glistening on her cheeks and her mouth open in a silent wail took his breath away.

Now the glow was behind him, and it grew stronger. Maurice back-winged, keeping himself between Angela and the spot on the wall. He looked over his shoulder and his wings stilled for a moment when he saw the moonlight-silvered, moss-covered stone wall and the silver gate solidifying and emerging from the wallpaper. Streamers of moonlight reached out through the ornate curlicues of the gate.

Angela's arms lifted and her hands stretched to touch the light.

"No way," he muttered. "Don't go into the light, Angie-baby."
~~~~~

Maurice had no idea if it was an old wives' tale, warning not to wake a sleepwalker, but he wasn't going to take a chance on startling her. Especially not when Angela was interwoven with whatever discord had disturbed the sleeping house. It had to be done slowly, gently. No question that it had to be done.

First step was to get her away from the stairs and back her away from the light before those gates opened and she stepped into that mass of shadows and moonlight behind them.

"Okay, let's hope the butterfly effect is real," he muttered. He put his back to Angela and his wings into high gear. Sweat immediately popped out on his forehead as he concentrated on staying in place in mid-air, while generating a strong gust of air. He flapped until his back muscles ached, and then he took a chance and looked over his shoulder.

He let out a whoop of triumph. Angela had backed away a good five or six steps. The tears had dried and her mouth had closed. As he watched, her hands dropped down to her sides again.

"Yes, yes, yes," he muttered, as the glow in the wallpaper faded away. Maurice moved closer to Angela and held onto the bannister for a better anchor. He put his back to her and resumed flapping, pushing her away from the landing and toward the open door of her apartment.

The glow in the wallpaper faded, but he was disappointed and a little frightened to see the gate and stone wall were still visible. At least they had been reduced to two-dimensional. They were part of the wallpaper now, like a mural. Somehow, he didn't think that was a good thing.

"Maurice?" Angela inhaled sharply. He turned to face her and gladly let his aching wings fold up against his back. "What--" She rubbed at her face and raked her fingers through her hair. "Did you see the gate and the moonlight?"

"It's okay. The gate didn't open. Go back to bed, Angie-baby. You're okay."

He considered calling Holly and begging her to hurry over here and look after Angela. Maurice had never felt so furious about his shrunken state as he did at that moment. What Angela needed was for someone big and strong to scoop her up in his arms and hold her until the color came back to her face.

"No, I am not okay." She stumbled as she turned around and

headed back to her quarters. She wrapped her arms around herself and glanced once over her shoulder before stepping through the door. "Would you call Asmondius? Ask him to come as soon as it's convenient for him?"

"You got it." Maurice snapped off a salute and was relieved to get a flicker of a smile from her. He waited until she stepped into her kitchen and filled the teakettle with water, before he swooped down to the main room and slapped the Wishing Ball into life.

Maurice wasn't surprised when the Wishing Ball awakened immediately. After all this time, if it wasn't sentient in its own magic-soaked way, the dark rainbow-swirled globe was aware in some elemental level. Or perhaps the disturbance in the magic woven through Divine's Emporium had awakened it so it didn't resist him. The call went through to Asmondius immediately, and he was grateful when the powerful Fae answered personally, instead of the answering mode.

"I don't have any new news for you, lad," Asmondius said. "But there have been reports of disturbances in the energy levels of every dimension that has some connection to Divine's Emporium. What kind of trouble have you been facing out there?"

He grew stern and didn't ask a single question as Maurice related Ethan's visit, what Lanie had seen and sensed, and the reaction in the very soil and air of Neighborlee to the presence of Wolcott and the punishment leveled by the Hounds. He shook his head, his mouth pressed flat and stern, when Maurice told him about Angela sleepwalking, and the gate that had tried to manifest through the wall where no dimensional gate belonged.

"I'll be there immediately. I suggest you not leave Angela alone until she is completely recovered."

Maurice didn't even waste time with a salute. He leaped up into the air and pushed his aching wings for top speed. Angela was pouring the boiling water into her big ceramic teapot painted with dragons and unicorns when he flew into her kitchen. Maurice suddenly found those images disturbing. Her color was practically normal. She had pulled out two teacups and the dollhouse tea set Maurice used. She had set the table in the front room with cookies, sugar-dusted cubes of Turkish delight, and dark chocolate bark.

"He's on his--" Maurice flinched and looked over his shoulder when he felt the transportation globe opening up in the wall next to his cupboard. "Way," he finished.

Angela picked up a shawl and wrapped it around herself, over her nightgown. She settled down at the table as Asmondius stepped through the globe. She said nothing as the Fae man stopped halfway to the table, looked her over head to foot, three times, and held out both his hands. She immediately gave her hands into his grasp. Maurice hovered, despite the ache in his back, because he knew he wouldn't be able to hold still if he landed. Not while the two of them just looked at each other, perfectly still, unblinking, and the air fairly crackled with silent communication.

"The time has come," Angela said, when Asmondius released her hand and sat down in front of the other full-size teacup. Both of them turned and looked somberly at Maurice.

"What? Time for what?" Maurice's voice cracked, and he wasn't ashamed of it.

"Surely it can't be that bad," Asmondius said. "Not to insult you, Maurice. You've come a long way. You're a proud example of how the Fae should have been for centuries in our interaction with Humans. But the exigency to bring it about..." He shook his head.

"Bring what about?" He barely restrained himself from shouting. Despite his size, Maurice knew he could shove both of them, and the table, against the far wall with the force of his bellow, if he wanted. Or needed.

"He doesn't know?"

"Why frighten him?" Angela shook her head and held her hand out to Maurice when he opened his mouth again. This time to shout. "For several months now, Asmondius and I have considered it a distinct possibility to have you take my place if something should happen to me."

"Take your place? If something happened to you?" Maurice landed hard, stomped across the table to stand in front of Angela's teacup, and braced himself on the lip of it. "You're not sick or anything, are you? Asmondius--come on--me? Take care of Divine's?"

"Ah, now see, that's the best indication of your new maturity and wisdom, and the appropriateness of choosing you as the next guardian and liaison. Let us hope, however, that the need never arises." Asmondius tipped up the lid on the teapot and sniffed at the steam rising from it. "Almost ready. No, lad, we don't want

Angela to leave, not the least because the circumstances requiring her to step down as guardian of the shop and all the dimensional doorways it guards would be heartbreaking. I'm pleased that you do see it as taking care of the shop, rather than running it. A subtle difference, yet a vast one. All in perception."

"So the Council approves of it? Of me staying here and taking care of things?" He shook his head. "Come on, Angie-baby, it can't be that bad. All the stuff we've been going through. You're not--you're not sick or anything, are you? Because yeah, maybe you need a break, there's a lot of rotten stuff happening all of a sudden, but-- No, this place would shrivel up and die without you. And put me in charge of protecting it all?" He shuddered, wanting to make a joke, but the fear and sickness coiling in his gut was too strong.

"I am under attack," Angela said quietly. "Not the shop, though it most certainly has been through the decades, the centuries... But this time I am the target, specifically. I thought they were attacking the shop by trying to destroy me, first, but... The sleepwalking tonight, the dreams I've been having..." She rubbed at her face and wrapped her shawl tighter around her shoulders.

"Asmondius, there's a new doorway in the wall of the landing on this floor. There shouldn't be one there. I didn't call it. I can't feel any life, any power on the other side of it, yet something calls me in my dreams and pulls me to enter. Maurice nearly tore his wings off tonight, keeping me from going through the gate."

"Excuse me." Asmondius got up and quietly hurried out of Angela's quarters.

Maurice wanted to go with him, to talk privately, to watch him study the doorway, but he wanted and needed to stay with Angela. Suddenly, she looked fragile. She looked mortal.

"Oh, Maurice, I do love you," Angela said, on a sigh that sounded like it tried to turn into laughter.

"Heh, don't tell Holly, okay? The chick is dangerous when she's jealous. You don't want to get a librarian riled at you." He settled down on the edge of Asmondius' saucer and crossed his arms on his knees. His attempt at a joke fell so flat, he couldn't have tripped over it if he tried.

"I'm flattered that you're so worried about me, scared to have me leave, and yes, I'm proud that you're frightened of the responsibility. And it's rather funny that you haven't thought of the most important part of you becoming the guardian of this place."

"Besides the entire town being in a whole heap of trouble to be stuck with me?"

"If you are assigned here, you and Holly can be together."

He forgot to breathe for a few seconds. His face warmed, to the point that his ear points burned.

"I think it would be very wise to designate her co-guardian. All the time she spends here has given her a good exposure to magic. And she is a Lost Kid, don't forget. It wouldn't be hard for her to soak up enough magic, living here with you, that she could conceivably have as long a life as you at full power."

"Oh, yeah, now make me really feel guilty. I'd rather give up all my magic altogether to be with Holly, than have anything happen to you, Angela."

"Let us hope it does not come to that." Asmondius came back into the room, picked up the teapot and poured for the three of them. The entire time, his mouth pressed flat in serious thought.

"Well?" Angela said, when he had reached for the cream, turned it amber, and poured half the pitcher into his cup, which expanded to accommodate the liquid.

And still Asmondius stared down into the creamy golden depths without speaking.

"It's bad news, huh? Maybe Big Ugly is trying to sneak in through the back door?" Maurice offered. He scurried across the table with his cup and held it under the spout of the cream pitcher to catch a single drop that hung suspended there, growing larger by the second until it was ready to fall like a ripe peach.

"No, it is not the nightmare sleeping in the cellar of the town." Asmondius levitated five cubes of sugar into his cup and slowly stirred it around by swirling his finger in the air. "I am unsure exactly what waits in that garden beyond the gates, but it is not inimical to you, Angela."

"It called me and pulled me to it in my sleep." She picked up her cup to sip it plain. "I would not call that friendly. Nothing has caused me to move against my will, without my knowledge or even consciousness of it, in...well, centuries."

Maurice swallowed hard, sensing Angela had been about to confess she could not remember any time that she hadn't been in control, when something or someone else had moved her like a doll or a piece on a chessboard.

"Should I have let her go through the gates?" He settled down at his doll table with his cup.

"Indeed not." Asmondius shook his head, sipped, and shook his head again. "You need to go through those gates and banish those shadows and bring the garden back to life, Angela. I could sense that much. The gates are keyed to you. But you should not, must not, go through them except at the time of your choosing. And definitely not alone."

"Then who must go with me?" she asked.

"Ah, now that is the puzzle. All I can offer you--and even that is a guess, for me--is that you will know him or her or them, when the time is right."

Oh, yeah, that's a really big help, Maurice silently grumbled.

~~~~~

The next afternoon, a chill crawled under the door from the building hallway, through Ethan's office. He could have sworn the lights dimmed slightly, barely enough to be noticeable. Something rattled, just twice, inside his desk drawer. He opened it slowly, one hand ready to grab whatever moved. He fully expected an enormous bug, like one of the killer cockroaches from that totally hokey movie version of *Damnation Alley.*

Instead, he saw the Von Helados' talisman lying on the bottom of the drawer in among the pens and paper clips and chewing gum wrappers, instead of in the coffee mug where he had put it.

That shiver of warning raced up his back, wearing soccer cleats. He listened to his gut instinct, even though common sense and self-preservation said to ignore it. Every time he listened to his sense of danger, of truth and lies, and paid attention to the voice that whispered of what was about to happen, he scraped another layer off that heavy, solid stone wall he had built around his sanity to protect it from otherness.

Despite all that, he had to listen. He had the awful, aching suspicion that he had made a soul-destroying choice when he tried not to listen. His gut churned with the certainty it might be too late to start listening.

Using a pencil, he hooked the chain and lifted the talisman to deposit it back into the mug. Then he shoved wads of paper and erasers on top of it, closed the drawer, and sat back in his chair,
~~~~~

forcing his body into an appearance of relaxation. He was proud of himself that he didn't flinch when the door opened a few heartbeats later and the Von Helados seeped into the room like a black fog.

"We have found Annabelle," Mrs. Von Helado announced.

Ethan wondered for the first time why her sons or grandsons, whoever they were, didn't speak. Maybe they couldn't? Maybe they were drugged or hypnotized. Maybe they weren't even Human at all, but robots or big, nasty guard dogs dressed up to look Human.

With a force of will, he kept his face calm and shoved his suddenly ludicrous, wild imagination back into the cold, dark closet where he usually kept it chained.

"Congratulations. I guessed that you had other investigators working in other states. One of them located her for you?" He reached for the drawer pull, glad to return the talisman and get it out of his possession once and for all.

"Not at all. You're the only one with the right, shall we say, qualifications?" Mrs. Von Helado nodded once for punctuation. That gleam Ethan could only describe as malice flickered once in her eyes. "You helped us narrow down quite a few leads, discarding illusions and lies. We're grateful. We want you to come with us to Neighborlee, Ohio, to help us confront her, keep her under control." Her thin smile widened slightly.

Ethan thought of the grin of a shark.

"Neighborlee?" If he lied, pretended ignorance, they would sense it. Now was not the time to make them panic and act too quickly. "I know the town. I've done some work for a P.I. there."

"What do you think of the place? The atmosphere?"

"It's a small college town. Feels like Mayberry, but with computers." He shrugged. "Nothing to write home about."

That chill raced up his back when Mrs. Von Helado definitely looked pleased with his response.

What would she have done, what would she have said, if he confessed that the town made the hairs stand up on his arms and prickled his scalp? That he gave himself a headache ignoring the illusions, the lights and movements and sounds that surrounded him from the moment he drove over the border.

"We're preparing the paperwork to take Annabelle into custody. We will have medical support, if necessary, if she resists us. It is vital that she not escape us this time."

"You're sure she's there?" He thought of their sketch and how Angela had grown sick and weak at the sight of it. The sour smell when it burned. How it had resisted when he tried to tear it.

Had he alerted them to her presence by taking the sketch to Divine's Emporium?

No, that was weeks ago. They would have acted right away, wouldn't they, if the sketch and its Dorian Gray reversal trick had been the trigger, the alarm?

"We're very sure. Not entirely one hundred percent." She let out a dry whisper of a laugh. "Would you be so kind as to go ahead of us? Study her, perhaps talk to her? Do a little preliminary work for us? Lawyers take so much time completing what should be simple tasks. It would be comforting to me to have a little more assurance while we're being delayed by tiresome legal matters."

"Yeah, sure. Might save you some trouble, in the long run. Wouldn't that be kind of embarrassing if you showed up with custody papers, and you found out you were wrong?"

"Highly embarrassing. Mortally so." Those eyes sparked malice again, and amusement. "We need you to gather a little evidence that she is indeed in need of caretakers. Why don't you take that sketch we gave you, and compare it to her?"

That answered that question. The destruction of the sketch hadn't alerted them.

"Even better, see if she remembers the bauble we gave you." She inhaled sharply and licked her lips, a movement more reminiscent of a lizard than a cat. "You do still have it, don't you?"

"Close and safe." Ethan opened the drawer and cleared the impromptu plug out of the top of the mug without them seeing. His skin suddenly crawled at the thought of touching the chain. He picked up the mug and upended it onto his cluttered blotter.

"Perhaps you should wear it around your neck, so it seems very casual when you encounter her. Let her notice it naturally. See where it leads."

"What if she recognizes it and calls for the cops, claiming I stole it? What if she goes into hysterics over it?"

"She won't. Annabelle was never the hysterical type, despite her flaws, her mental problems." Again, that lizard-like flick of the tongue.

Ethan vowed never to wear that talisman. With all the things the lab had found coating the chain and the coin, the low-level radiation and Angela's reaction to the sketch, nothing in the world could convince him to let it touch his bare skin. Poison or mind-altering drugs or something else, something beyond his imagination, he wasn't taking any chances.

In less than ten minutes, it was done. He agreed with the Von Helados to meet here in his office in five days to report on what he had found and plan the next step in the campaign to retrieve poor, demented, helpless Anabelle. He fought to look relaxed as the grim little group left his office. Ethan listened to the thudding of his heart, willing it to slow and calm, and let him hear the sound of their footsteps in the hall and the bing of the elevator, meaning they had left his floor.

"It stops now," he whispered when he was sure he was alone.

If there was anyone in the world who was the polar opposite of the woman the Von Helados described to him, it was Angela.

He stuck to the timetable of the plan he had made with them. He stayed in his office clearing up loose ends, making arrangements to be away for a few days, and then went home at the end of the day. He made sure the talisman was in the mug and locked the drawer. There were only a few times in his career that Ethan hadn't trusted his clients. All the other incidents combined didn't add up to the wrongness, the certainty of lies and ulterior motives and threat he sensed from the Von Helados.

He had learned it was wise to always overestimate his enemy's capabilities. As in having him watched, followed, his phone bugged. He stopped at a drug store on his way home and used a pay phone, probably the only one in the entire city, to call Stanzer. Less than five minutes later, he hung up and continued on his way, feeling a little better with the knowledge that the other investigator had been warned, and he would warn Angela in turn.

Chapter Nine

"Mr. Jarrod." Angela was standing in front of the counter in the main room of the shop when Ethan walked in early the next morning, before Divine's Emporium had officially opened for the day. He would have thought she would have stayed behind it, putting the heavy marble barrier between them, like a shield.

"I don't suppose you'd be willing to call me by my first name?"

"Not quite yet. Yes, you are acting as a friend and ally, and John trusts you. But--"

"But you don't." He shrugged. "Fair enough. I guess it has to be earned. Especially after what happened last time."

"You say these people are preparing legal documents to take control over me?" She lifted one hand and rested it on a dark, rainbow-shimmering globe sitting on the counter. Ethan flinched when tendrils of multi-colored, pearly mist rose from the globe and wrapped around her fingers. Angela lifted one elegant eyebrow. "Do you see that?"

"I don't know what I see." He coughed to clear his throat of whatever made his voice turn into a rasp.

"You don't want to see. You're very good at not seeing," she half-whispered. "But this--everything that's happening--is pulling down all the barriers you've erected in your mind."

"Look, these people who claim to be your relatives sent me here to get evidence that you're crazy." He tried to laugh. It caught in his throat. "Don't give me that evidence."

"I'm not insane, but you could well be if you don't learn to believe. Or learn once and for all *not* to see all those things that dance at the edges of your sight and your imagination. I believe I feel sorry for you, Mr. Jarrod."

"That's a start at friendship, huh?" He looked around the shop, caught in wonder for a moment at the wonderful hodge-podge of treasures and junk. He even enjoyed the sensation that there was far more here than what he could see, as if a slight turn, a different angle of view, would reveal multiple doorways and stairs where no stairs or doors belonged, and upside-down rooms, like in an Escher drawing.

He dug his hands into his pockets just to have something to do. Something sticky and hot bit his fingertips. Ethan cursed and yanked his hand out. The talisman came with his hand and clattered to the ground.

It shouldn't have been in his pocket. How did it get out of that locked drawer? He planned to tell the Von Helados that she didn't react to it. That would be the truth, because how could she react to something she didn't see?

Angela sagged against the counter, staring at the talisman. The light coming from the globe darkened and the tendrils thinned.

"I did not bring that with me. I swear. I left it in my office. I don't know how--" He was babbling. He clamped his mouth shut.

"More proof of outside forces acting on us, using you in a desperate, brutal campaign." She shuddered.

Ethan took a step closer, positive she was going to pass out on him. He stopped with one foot in the air.

The talisman lying on the floor in front of him glowed with a weird, black light effect. Misty rainbow streaks trailed along the floor, floating toward the coin as if it sucked all the light into it.

"That's not good," he muttered. Images and ideas crashed through his head. Pictures of himself in a dozen different costumes and times and settings collided in his mind.

"Pick it up," Angela whispered.

"Are you crazy? The lab says there's something on it. I'm ready to believe it's some new drug."

"Ready to believe, but not quite? As long as you don't believe, you're safe."

"Believe in what?"

"I can't tell you. You might believe. Please!" Angela half-stumbled to a display rack on the other side of the counter, picked up a thickly embroidered scarf, and tossed it to him.

"I want some answers, lady." He wadded up the scarf and bent. Clashing images tore through him, warning him not to touch the talisman, and begging him to destroy it. But how?

"You'll have more answers than you'll ever need if you'll just do! What! I! Say!"

"Baby, you're beautiful when you snarl." He took a deep breath and reached down to pick up the necklace before he lost his nerve.

"Hey, Angela? What's going on? The whole top of the house is twisting like it wants to pull all the nails loose." A little man with gaudy, shining wings flew into the room and hovered in the air midway between Ethan and Angela.

Ethan froze, staring at the little man. He was close enough to make out the details of his clothes--a lavender polo shirt and khakis. The little man stared back, his face twisting in fury.

"What are you doing back here?" he growled, and despite his size, his voice made the room vibrate.

No, Ethan realized a moment later. The shaking, the vibrations, came from the coin, as the streaks of light spilling into it--sucked into it--grew thicker and darker.

"We have to get that out of here." Angela stumbled away from the counter, reaching for the talisman, holding another scarf in her hand.

One thing crystallized for Ethan in that moment. No matter what happened, Angela must not touch that thing. Not even with the insulation of the scarf. The world would shatter and crumble to dust if she did. He dove, reaching for the talisman, to get to it first.

The little man was closer. He went into a tailspin. The light trailing from his wings was sucked ahead of him into the talisman. He let out a yelp of triumph as he scooped it up by the chain.

Darkness erupted out of the coin and black light flared from the chain. It jolted up into the air, pulling the little man with it.

"Maurice, where are you taking it?" Angela shouted.

"Heck if I know. It's taking *me*!" Maurice shouted, his wings beating so furiously they were nearly invisible as he fought the pull of coin and chain. He was losing the tug-war as the talisman neared the doorway into the room.

"Let go!"

"I can't!"

A heartbeat later, it pulled him out and around the corner.

"It's going up the stairs." Angela staggered past Ethan.

He followed her, holding onto the scarf with a vague idea of grabbing the talisman and pulling the little man free. They raced up the stairs, with the talisman and its prisoner getting two steps further ahead of them with every one step they took.

"The painting room," Angela gasped, when muffled thuds

113

reverberated down to them from the fourth floor, just as they reached the third-floor landing. "Thank goodness, it's locked."

"Angela!" The shout came from above. "It's getting ready to blast--"

Black light erupted down the stairs in jagged waves as they reached the landing between the third and fourth floors. Angela leaped two stairs. Ethan twisted sideways and got ahead of her and reached the fourth floor in time to see a blackened door swing open and the talisman, pulling the little man, streak into the room.

"No, he can't go through," Angela said, as she stumbled onto the landing. "The paintings are spelled to block him. It's part of his exile. If it tries to pull him through--"

The panic on her face moved Ethan more than her words, which didn't make any conscious sense. What frightened him, though, was that on the gut level, he knew exactly what she feared, what she meant. He dove into the darkened room, taking a swing at the wall where he expected a light switch to be. It didn't come on.

The lack of light didn't matter. Black light lit the room in bursts every time the talisman slammed into the frame of a painting, like splatters from a triple-sized paint ball shot at the highest velocity. It ricocheted around the room, slamming against painting frames, knocking them out of their racks and off the walls and off the crates where they were propped up. It left a trail of black light, slapping Maurice against twice as many surfaces, still caught on the end of the chain trailing behind it.

Ethan lunged, barely remembering to use the hand insulated with the scarf, reaching to grab the chain. It led him on a wildcat dance around the room, banging into crates and dislodging paintings from their resting places.

He stumbled over a stack of paintings, knocking one out from behind another. Angela cried out warning as the talisman arched up to the ceiling and dove, slapping its captive against the high surface before dragging him down with it. The painting finished falling as if in slow motion, landing painted side facing up. The surface flared with blood-tinted light and the talisman penetrated with a splash as if it were water.

Ethan fell backward against a crate, staring, stunned when the canvas didn't break. The painting absorbed the talisman, and then the chain.

Maurice yelped as he hit the surface and a geyser of silver and gold and poisonous green sparkles hid him from view. His yelp turned into a howl of pain, and the sparkles grew thicker, higher, and took on an orange cast, as if the painting would burst into flames at any moment.

Angela went to her knees on the frame of the painting and reached into the eruption of light. Ethan had a flash of an image of her falling into the painting. He flung himself down on the other side of the frame and reached into that stinging, cold, fizzling power.

A noise like a sonic boom deafened him and blinding light erupted, flinging him and Angela backward against the walls, knocking over every painting that hadn't been toppled. Frames cracked and warped. Clouds of multi-colored dust gushed upward.

Ethan rubbed his eyes, trying to clear them, and dimly watched as several paintings went completely black, and then turned to empty, pristine canvas inside their broken frames.

He was surrounded with silence. He spent a few seconds checking himself. Nothing broken, nothing torn. No blood. No burns, despite the smell of scorch, thick and bitter in the air. Then he caught a dim thrumming. He nearly laughed in relief to recognize his slowing pulse in his ears. At least he wasn't deaf. When he turned over and got to his knees, he saw Angela kneeling over a man's body sprawled across the painting on the floor. The canvas on this one hadn't turned white. It was shredded and blackened. Thin tendrils of smoke curled up in the air.

The talisman softly glowed a menacing purple hue among the ashes.

"Maurice. Maurice, wake up," Angela sobbed, her voice growing stronger as Ethan's hearing returned.

He knelt next to her, shaking all over, feeling scorched and oxygen-deprived and aching. He stared at Maurice, now over six feet tall, bruised and pale, with his clothes scorched and burned in some spots, torn in others, and a faint haze of smoke seeping from his flesh. The soles of his sneakers were completely melted away, just the scorched uppers remaining on his feet. Somehow, the pointed ears revealed by his scorched, smoking hair were the least of all the impossibilities and surprises.

"Is it safe to move him?" he asked. "Get him out of this smoke, into clear air."

Angela's head snapped up and she stared at him, eyes wide, made enormous by the tears glistening in them. It amused him for a moment to realize she had completely forgotten he was there.

"Yes." She swallowed hard and rubbed the tears from her eyes with the back of her hand. She smeared some of the ash from the painting across her cheeks. "Yes, please, we should move him, make him comfortable." A trembling exhale escaped her, evidence of sobs she fought. "Oh, Maurice, what do I tell Holly if anything happens to you?"

Ethan took most of Maurice's weight, but Angela supported his feet and guided them down the three flights of stairs. They ended up in the furniture room, and settled him, still unconscious, on a long, old swayback sofa.

"Wouldn't he be more comfortable in his own bed?" Ethan said, when Angela produced a basin of herb-scented water and a soft cloth from nowhere.

"Maurice's bed isn't even big enough for one foot, let alone all of him." She shook her head, frowning as she swabbed the smeared ashes off his forehead, and then pressed the cloth against his throat, his wrists, and wiped his face again, wringing out the cloth each time.

"Oh. Right." He shuddered, remembering with an odd sense of calm he couldn't quite understand. Until that geyser of light, Maurice had been as tall as his palm, and flew on big, glittery, Hollywood-gaudy wings.

They both jumped when a banging sounded at the front door. A moment later Ethan saw the light ripple through the room. He had a sense of the light doing that through the entire shop. The front door slammed open and the sound of running feet came toward them through the shop. A plump young woman with ginger-tinted hair and pale, round cheeks hurtled into the room.

"What happened?" she demanded, and slid to her knees next to the sofa, reaching for Maurice's hands.

Ethan figured it was a good bet this was the Holly Angela had mentioned.

"How did you know?" Angela asked.

"I felt it. Like someone pulled hard on something I was holding and couldn't let go of, and then just before it snapped, they let go and it rebounded on me." She tugged on a braided cord hanging around her neck and brought out a teardrop-shaped pendant. A smoky haze coated it, obscuring the glossy white surface. "What did he do?"

"Feels like I sunburned the inside of my skull and my skin," Maurice said, his voice a creaky whisper. He didn't move, didn't open his eyes, but he winced when Holly pressed his hand to her cheek.

"A very apt description." Angela scrubbed her eyes clear of tears with the heel of her hand. She stood up and gestured for Ethan to come with her. "Holly, keep him from doing anything until I send for help."

"Help? What kind of help? Maurice, so help me, if you tried to break that curse ahead of time and make the council listen..."

"The exact opposite." She bent and squeezed Holly's shoulder. "He was playing the hero to the extreme. I fear he stepped into a trap meant for me. Keep him quiet, would you?"

"Don't worry," Maurice said. "Couldn't get me to move to save my life. Aww, honey, don't cry."

Ethan followed Angela to the main room of the shop. He felt as if he walked about an inch above the floor. All sounds and colors were muted, yet at the same time all his senses had an added dimension. The question was if the change was in him or the shop. Maybe he had been scorched inside and out, as Maurice had so aptly put it, and something clogging his senses had been burned away.

"Do you have it?" Angela asked. She flinched when Ethan brought the talisman out of his pocket.

He kept the scarf between it and his skin, and flinched again, remembering how it had bit his fingers when he thoughtlessly put his hand in his pocket. If he hadn't reacted, if he had left it in his pocket, none of the last half hour would have happened.

"It looks dead, or at least quiet for now. Who gave this to you, and why?" She shook her head when Ethan opened his mouth to respond. "Hold that thought. I have to send for help."

She turned to the dark, iridescent globe sitting on the counter and pressed one hand to the top curve. The colors slowly swirled, gaining speed the longer she spoke. "This is an emergency call to Asmondius of the Disciplinary Council, and a request for medical assistance for Maurice, assigned on parole to Divine's Emporium. He has been seriously injured, caught between a dimensional transport curse and the barrier spells woven into his exile. He is back to his normal size, but--"

"But you're not sure if anything else is normal?" A wizened, silver-bearded man in a violent purple sweat suit flickered into being four steps behind her. "Believe me, my dear lady, the alarm went off the moment the spell was destroyed in such a brutal manner. I came as soon as I got the coordinates. Where is the boy?"

Ethan sat down. He had to, with the way the floor seemed to be rolling like a stormy sea under his feet. He landed at a white wrought iron bistro table and waited for Angela to come back from showing the old man to the furniture room. The worst part of all this was the feeling, growing stronger every moment, that everything should have seemed perfectly normal to him. And that didn't make any sense.

"You'd feel better if you gave yourself permission to believe," Angela observed, when she came back into the room.

"Believe what?" Ethan flinched at the volume of his voice, which seemed to echo off the ceiling, the display of dishes on one side of the room, and the windows.

"Coffee?" She narrowed her eyes and tipped her head to one side for a moment. Her lips flicked into and out of a smile. "I can't... read you, for some reason. It's odd. Refreshing, but odd. What kind of coffee would you like?"

"Black. As strong as you can make it." He snorted and rested his face in his hands, rubbing at his eyes. He felt as if he had been awake six days in a row, on his feet the whole time. "I don't suppose you could make it half whiskey?"

"Let's start with coffee, and if you need it, I'll find something stronger." Just moments later, she set a cup down on the table in front of him. She took the seat opposite him with her own cup.

Both cups were twice the normal size. Ethan snorted, sparsely amused to see the liquid in his cup was so deep black it looked thick, as if he couldn't stick his finger through the surface. Definitely the way he liked his coffee. He took a sip, holding the cup in both hands, and was astonished to find it was scalding hot.

"How did--" No, he didn't want to know how she dispensed coffee hot enough to be fresh, but thick enough to have been condensing in a pot on the back burner for a week. He took a swallow and waited until the heat and the extra-strength caffeine jolted through his system. Then he opened his eyes, sat back, watching Angela sip coffee that was nearly white with cream, and started talking.

He liked how she didn't react when he told her everything about the Von Helados, their claims about her, the information they had given him, the blank circle with Neighborlee at the center. He told her about the lab report on the talisman, and even told her about the time he was sure it had jumped out of the mug where he kept it.

She watched him, face serene, eyes hooded, and sipped slowly. Until he told her how the Von Helados had showed up in his office again with their plans to file papers to take her into custody.

"What date was this, exactly?" She slowly, carefully put her cup down on the table.

Ethan saw the first reaction in her when he told her.

"I should have known, should have realized. We had an... well, let's just call it an incident, here. The shield around our town was threatened, momentarily weakened or compromised, I suppose. Until that point, they have been prevented from entering, limited to working through tricks and outside agents. If this Von Helado woman is who I suspect... The way you describe her ... if she was not destroyed in our last battle, then she was drained, shriveled to the woman you saw.

"Now, with the disruption from inside the shield, they believe they are able to enter Neighborlee. They were using you as their advance scout, and the coin ... oh, yes, that coin is a telling point. They tried to use spelled, cursed coins earlier this year to infiltrate, to cloud people's minds. There is no telling what that coin was meant to do to you, if you took her suggestion and wore it. You might have granted them permission to use you, to attack me." She shook her head. "The question still remains, are they after me, specifically? Or am I just a tool, a means to break down the gate that prevents them from invading other realms?"

"They wanted you to get pulled into that painting." Ethan nearly laughed at how ridiculous that statement was on the surface, yet he knew it was the simple truth.

"A very unfriendly painting. Many people through the

generations have tried to destroy it and were destroyed themselves. I suppose it is irony that the very magic sent to imprison me there was strong enough to eliminate at least one threat."

She sat up and glanced at the doorway, as the old man appeared again. "How is he, Doctor?"

"You have a very sick young hero on your hands." He shook his head. The starkness in his eyes sent an answering throb through Ethan. He had seen men look more hopeful as they watched a buddy bubble his life away, with a dozen bullet holes in his chest.

"The inimical magic wound itself around his inborn magic to have a strong enough grip to pull him through the dimensional doorway. However, the conditions of Maurice's exile were also interwoven with the core of his magic. Part of the limitations on him, you see. The tug of war set up a friction and unraveled some things that I thought could never be unraveled." He shook his head and *tsked* a few times. "I just don't know. Be thankful he was returned to his normal size and those wings were removed, otherwise I'm mighty fearful he might have been stuck that way for the rest of his life."

"Ah..." Angela blinked a threat of tears out of her eyes. "What should I do for him?"

"The best medicine is that young lady holding his hand right now. But some heavy-duty cosseting wouldn't be amiss. I'll be back in a few days to see if there's been any change. Human-style analgesics, lots of chocolate. And I'd stock up on a couple crates of diet cherry cola to let him drown his sorrows." He bowed to her, stepped back, and vanished in a swirl of purple sparkles.

"Does that happen a lot?" Ethan didn't even bother rubbing his eyes, in the vague hope he was imagining all this.

"It's almost normal around here, yes." Angela shook her head and looked at the talisman, lying on the table between them. "If the struggle killed this, then the Von Helados know you met me and the curse was triggered. If it is only sleeping... You have to get it out of here before it wakes up. It is so old, so steeped in evil magic, it could be aware. Awake. If it knows it failed, it will try something else. Cause whatever damage it can. It could penetrate the shield from the inside and let its masters come through." She shuddered delicately, her features wrinkling for a moment in mixed pain and revulsion.

Something hot and angry stirred to life in Ethan's chest. Angela should never shudder like that, to feel a moment's fear or anguish. He hated the Von Helados for what they were trying to do to her, and for using him to weaken her for their attack.

She wasn't the kind of woman who needed protection and constant tending, like a hothouse flower. He suspected she had many allies, people who would lay their lives on the line to defend her, and yet never consider themselves her defenders, because they saw her as strong, omniscient, eternally serene.

She might not need him, but Ethan wanted to protect her. Yet everything he had seen in the last two hours was beyond his experience, so what good could he do her?

"Could you leave?" he said finally, when he envisioned picking her up in his arms, carrying her out to his car and driving to an airport to get her out of the country, if necessary.

"I defend this place as much as it defends me." She briefly rested her hand over his on the table, little more than brushing her fingertips across the back of his hand.

The contact sent sparks through him, starting something fizzing in the back of his mind, in the dark, locked places. It stirred something in his chest that he thought was long dead and cold, turned to dust from lack of use.

"Then let me stay and help." He couldn't believe he had said that. "What little good I can do, considering all the..." He gestured around the shop. The words stuck in his throat.

"The magic? The otherness?" A sparkle touched her eyes for a moment. Did she laugh at him, or did she understand his struggle?

"I'm pretty good with a gun. And other weapons." For some odd reason, he remembered the words of that woman at the newspaper office, the last time he had been in Neighborlee. She had called him a knight, a slayer of dragons. The mental image of a long, heavy sword in his hands, slashing and smashing and hacking his way through enemies, made him feel good. Useful.

"This danger, these enemies, are not the kind who can be dealt with using Human weapons." She stood, and Ethan was instantly on his feet. "Thank you, but the greatest service you can do me is to take that poisoned thing out of here, back to its -- no, not to its makers. Why give them a weapon to use again? Just get it out of here. Any poison inside our borders could be our undoing."

Ethan drove away a short time later, after stopping at Stanzer's office and consulting with him. If the Von Helados realized what he had done and punished him, he wanted to make sure Angela was warned, and she and her allies could be prepared for whatever happened next.

He couldn't help feeling as if he had been punished for something that wasn't his fault. That he was a child who had been sent away for the crimes of his parents or his siblings. An ache shot through him the moment he crossed the border, leaving Neighborlee, but it didn't diminish with time and distance. If anything, it settled deep inside and became a part of him. And it stirred an anger he hadn't allowed himself to feel in years.

~~~~~

"Is he gone?" Maurice's voice was slightly louder, stronger, but still a croak, as if his throat had been scorched. Amazing how sharp his ears had grown when they were the only sense he could use without feeling that sunburn prickling that made him want to dive into something cool and thick and wet. The problem was that he needed to do it to the *inside* of his head and the underside of his skin.

"Gone." Angela stepped into the room, her footsteps stopping at the foot of the couch where Maurice usually woke up on his days of full-size freedom from wings.

"Can't trust him."

"I know." She sighed. Maurice opened one eye and saw the faint lines around her mouth and eyes, the shadows in her eyes, the weariness. "Until he is willing to see, to hear, to believe, he will remain their tool."

"This might help," Holly announced, scurrying into the room. "Angela, I hope you don't mind, but--" She gestured with a slight lift of the tray in her hands, holding ice cream and cold cream and sunglasses.

"Everything here is at Maurice's disposal." Angela stepped over to the other wall and pulled a little table forward, for Holly to put the tray on. "Doctor's orders are heavy-duty cosseting."

"He even prescribed a bath of cherry cola." Maurice tried to snicker, but it hurt his throat. Holly was instantly there, before he could finish wincing, offering a big spoonful of ice cream. He moaned through the blissfully cold and creamy mouthful,
~~~~~

swallowed, and closed his eyes, hating the tears glistening in hers.

"Maurice, what exactly did he--"

"He didn't say anything exactly, but we both know the verdict."

"Your magic is gone, isn't it?" Holly whispered.

"For now," Angela said. "And since this is entirely out of the doctor's experience, we have no real idea when it will come back."

"If it will come back," Maurice corrected. He opened his eyes, despite the ache from normal light. "Looks like you're stuck with me, babe."

"No, you're stuck with me." Holly slid the sunglasses on over his eyes and bent down to kiss him.

His lips stung a little at the pressure, but Maurice didn't care. He knew better than to tell Holly or Angela right now that the trade-off was well worth it. Just like the proposal to have him take over the guardianship of Divine's Emporium, this situation solved his problem of how to stay with Holly. With his magic burned out of him, he was mortal.

Well worth it, he told himself again. He settled back to let Holly feed him ice cream and smooth cold cream over his tingling, prickling skin to sooth it. He planned to enjoy all the pampering he could get before he had to learn how to live as an ordinary mortal.

~~~~~

By noon, Maurice couldn't stand lying still. Especially with people coming in and out of Divine's to shop. He had never noticed it being so busy on a weekday before. Then again, he had never been visible, flat on his back on the sofa in the furniture room, with people coming in to look at a piece they'd been thinking about for days and stopping short at the sight of him. He knew the shop would grow a room for him the moment Angela asked, but he just didn't want to move. He also didn't want to find out that he couldn't feel magic at work. Even when his personal magic had been shrunk, he could still feel others' magic at work. Until now.

Maybe it was being visible that bothered him the most. He had grown used to, and grown to like, being able to zip around the shop, hovering near the ceiling, listening in on the fascinating and strange and sometimes totally inane conversations of customers. All while entirely invisible and inaudible to ninety-nine percent of the people he encountered on a daily basis. Now, he had to make eye contact and conversation and his body suddenly felt huge and
~~~~~

slow and awkward. When he finally got up on his feet and got moving, he always seemed to be where someone wanted to look or stand.

He couldn't even complain to Angela because the shop wasn't empty for more than two minutes at a time. Someone always wanted her help, or they loitered in the main room where Maurice perched on a stool and leaned on the counter. People were a lot more tolerant of or oblivious to weird things in Neighborlee than in the rest of the Human realm, but the things he needed to discuss with Angela might just push the envelope for anyone who overheard them.

"You're not invisible anymore," Angela said, when he tried to bring up the subject for the fourth time, and finally succeeded. "Think about it. Think about all the people you've wanted to make friends with. And all the people you wouldn't want to be friends with, who would be terrified at all the inside information you have on them." Her eyes sparkled and her lips twitched against a smile that struggled to break free.

Right on cue, the bells over the door jangled and a horde of children streamed into the shop, herded by three adult caretakers from Eden, the community center. Obviously, it was break time at the daycare center. Judging from the splatters of paint on little faces and hands and gobs of paste and colored tissue paper in their hair and stuck to their clothes, it was the art class this time. Yesterday it had been the peewee wiffleball class.

"Need help riding herd?" Maurice slid off the stool as three-quarters of the children thundered up to the counter, calling out the candy they wanted. How come those little voices sounded louder and there seemed to be more children when he was full-size?

Chapter Ten

Maurice had fun for the next half hour or so, until he ran out of energy and had to sit down, retreating to the quiet of Angela's quarters. During that time, he sauntered around the shop, watching out for the children, keeping them from wandering away from their harried teachers, addressing them by name, pointing out their favorite candy, asking about their friends or their pets or older brothers and sisters. It amazed him that the children seemed to know him before Angela introduced him as Mr. Maurice, who was going to help with the shop for a while. Their teachers, however, were a little stunned at this complete stranger showing up who knew as much about the children in their care as they did.

"My theory is that the children have seen you all this time, flying around and watching over them," Angela said, when they had settled down in her apartment that evening after the shop closed. "They're able to not only believe in magic and other worlds, but sometimes find the doorways and trigger the magic. They're closer to that state of mind and soul where they know how to listen to the guiding voice inside them."

"Jiminy Cricket," Maurice muttered, and got a gentle slap against the back of his head from Holly.

She had joined them for dinner, hurrying over as soon as the library closed. "In the original story, Pinocchio stomped on the cricket," Holly said. "So you be careful."

"Hey, there's no way anybody'd mistake me for a cricket anymore," he protested, grinning.

"Thank goodness." Angela shook her head at their foolery, smiling. "I wouldn't be surprised if some of the children approach you in the next few days, asking how come you're not flying anymore, where your wings went, and how you grew up so fast."

"Keep an eye on those special ones?" he guessed.

Naturally, the talk turned to the news Ethan had brought, and speculation about the Von Helados. Was Mrs. Von Helado their nemesis, Kerri, shriveled by her last defeat? The cursed coin they had tried to use against Angela was too similar to the coins used to control the Homework Hub women, in an attempt to not only allow a pedophile to plant roots in Neighborlee, but perhaps help rebel Fae to attack the shield from the inside.

Maurice found it hard to think back to those few minutes of struggle as the coin tried to pull him through the painting. He fought to remember the sensations, the different frequencies of magic, to try to identify the source.

"It's nothing I ever encountered when I was doing the tourist thing through different dimensions," he said, after working himself into a headache, trying to describe the experience to Angela and Holly. "That doesn't mean a whole lot. There are a lot of places I've never been. Maybe you should call the doc back and have him do another scan on me, see if he can pick up any of the frequencies or resonances or whatever that scorched me, and try to match to anything recorded in the Ether Lexicon."

"Wish I could get a look at that," Holly said, more thinking aloud than actually responding to the discussion.

"Oh, honey, you'd have a great time. It's as big as it needs to be. If knowledge is power, when the Lexicon materializes for you, I bet it's bigger than this house," Maurice offered. He laughed when she blushed bright red.

"What worries me," Angela said after a few moments, when their humor faded and the seriousness of the discussion returned, "is that I'm more sure than ever this is a reaction to that battle with Wolcott. I think the protective barrier around Neighborlee... I don't know, slipped? Faded? Blanked out for a few seconds? What I hope is that something leaked out."

"As opposed to?" Holly said. From the grimness around her mouth, Maurice thought she suspected the same thing that he and Angela seemed to.

"Something got inside the shield," Maurice offered, when Angela shook her head and sipped at her tea instead of answering. "Something snuck in, and when the shield went back into place, it was quiet enough that the computer kids haven't noticed yet." He referred to London and Sherwood, the Artificial Intelligences who monitored and tried to bolster the town's shield.

"The sensors were scorched sufficiently to not notice any changes," Angela said with a nod. "Or... Well, everything is so focused on keeping track of Big Ugly… Well, it's tunnel vision. Even after the latest mess with the doppelgangers and that Kerri woman, we're so used to focusing on one enemy, all our defenses have become blind to new, small, quiet intruders."

"So what do we do?" Holly said.

"Warn our friends to be alert, to expand their search parameters, to look for anything that seems to fit, yet doesn't quite."

"Heh." Maurice hooked his thumb at his own chest. "That fits a lot of the people and things in this town, starting with me."

"You fit, Maurice." Her smile turned warmer, yet with a weariness that sent an ache through his chest at the same time. "You've made a place for yourself here. Now all that needs doing is figuring out exactly what you want to do."

All? Yeah, easier said than done. Maurice kept his thoughts to himself. He was just glad to be able to sit here with his arm around Holly, feeling nothing but tired. The scorched, itchy sensation inside his skull and skin had faded. For the most part.

And maybe he was a little proud of himself, too. Sure, two years ago he had been on a vengeance quest to right the wrongs and squash the bullies. Sacrificing himself, risking his life and a chance at being with Holly was much more fulfilling. Granted, he was relieved he hadn't lost either. Knowing Angela was safe and Divine's hadn't been damaged and the dimensional doorways were safe was well worth the possibly permanent loss of his magic.

He knew what he wanted to do: settle down with Holly and learn how to live entirely in her world. Angela would offer him a job at Divine's if he wanted it. The question was if he really wanted it. Did he want to spend the rest of his life within smelling and touching and tasting distance of all the magic he had lost, and would never have again? Maybe he needed to make the break. Not leave Neighborlee, but take the big step and look at the rest of the town. What kind of job could he do?

Didn't Humans need a lot of ridiculous paperwork to get around in the modern world? He would have to learn about cell phones and driving cars and working bank machines and remote controls.

Finally, he put the consideration aside for later. He was tired, and more than willing to let Angela and Holly follow doctor's orders and cosset him for the rest of the evening.

Still, despite his resolve to be proud of what he had done, and not regret his loss, he still felt a pang when Angela announced Divine's had recovered from the shock and strain of that morning and had budded a room at the end of the hall to give him a full-size bedroom and bedroom furniture. He could have done it himself that morning, before getting scorched. He wondered if he would ever be able to talk to the shop again, and have it respond or if he would always have to ask Angela to intervene.

"Dream about us," Holly whispered, as she kissed him goodnight on the front porch.

"Try to stop me," he choked out, managing to keep his voice almost normal. His face actually hurt as he kept up the smile, standing under the porch light, watching Holly as she hurried down the sidewalk and vanished into the darkness.

He wouldn't be able to visit Holly's dreams anymore, would he?

Now he had something to regret.

"You are just starting your recovery," Angela said, as he stepped back into the shop and pulled the door closed behind him. "If you believe you will recover at least some of your magic, that is half the battle."

"But what if--" Maurice couldn't finish, didn't want to finish the rest of his question, even in his thoughts. He wasn't at all ashamed when a shuddering sigh escaped him, turning into tears.

Angela wrapped her arms around him, pulling his head down to her shoulder. It didn't feel at all ridiculous to let his few tears soak her shoulder, even though he was taller than her and had to bend down to do it.

~~~~~

The question tried to slither up from the back of his mind several times through the following day. Maurice pushed the depressing thought aside by repeating positive thoughts to himself: *I will heal. I will have magic again. I will. I believe.* And he fought back with action. He carried crates of new inventory up from the cellar, encouraged when the magically sealed doors of the two lower cellars were not only visible to him, but opened for him without his having to ask. He filled shelves and rearranged the furniture room, and grinned at the old sofa where he had awakened on the days he was full-size.
~~~~~

He stayed out of the way, though, when the children spilled through the shop in swarms, depending on what activity group had just ended for the day. Their noise and their multitude of questions and simply the change in air pressure inside the shop bothered him, revealing that his scorched senses, physical and magical, hadn't fully recovered.

"Get out of here and face the full-size world," Angela said, shaking her head, when he was chased out of yet another room by a tidal wave of children in search of treasures and treats. She laughed, finally sounding like her normal self, as Maurice sidled around the children and beat a hasty retreat for the front door.

He skidded to a stop after only four steps.

A display of jewelry caught his eye, sunlight sparkling off faceted edges and casting rainbows across the room. Maurice frowned. Something about the angle of the light seemed wrong. A moment of thought showed him the answer. It was noon. The sun shouldn't be at that low angle at this time of the day.

He looked around, following light that streamed in strong and golden through a window that ordinarily wasn't there. The view through the sheer curtains revealed a forest-ringed meadow where unicorns and peacocks strolled.

Maurice grinned, wondering if anyone else could see that window and what lay beyond it. If most other people couldn't, that was a good sign for him, wasn't it? He glanced over his shoulder at Angela. She was busy holding a glass jar of multi-colored licorice whips for a little girl who could barely see over the counter. Still, she must have felt Maurice's gaze, because she glanced up for a moment and winked, and then tipped her head in the direction of the jewelry display in the middle of that beam of sunlight.

Maurice might have been without usable magic for the foreseeable future, but he could take a magical hint. He sauntered over to the display case and nearly staggered at what he saw.

On Valentine's Day, he and Holly had gone deep sea diving in her dream and discovered a sunken treasure ship. Among all the gold and jewels and ornate chests and antiquities, Holly had found a small crystal box. Inside was a ring. That ring now sat in the display case, encased in sunlight, with the crystal box propped open. The band was three silver strands, braided, and the knot held a sapphire surrounded with tiny diamonds. In the dream, Holly had taken this ring and left the rest of the treasure behind. Maurice had promised himself that someday, he would find a ring just like it for her to wear when they were both awake.

He didn't have to ask Angela. The light and the window were evidence she knew about the ring and what it meant to him and Holly. Maurice took the crystal box and ring from the display and turned, bowing grandly to Angela. She blew him a kiss and gestured him out with a shooing motion.

"Who's that, Miss Angela?" the little girl buying licorice chirped.

"That's Mr. Maurice. He's going to be living here now. You'll like him a lot. He tells wonderful stories."

"Oh, thanks a lot, Angie-baby," Maurice said as he hurried out the front door. Then he laughed. Actually, he knew a couple hundred stories he could tell the children to amaze and amuse them. It would be easy, because most of them were true.

Maybe he would make a living as a storyteller. Why not? He had to find a way to make a living, the Human way. He had already decided he couldn't become a magician like Alexi and Megan. He might have fun doing investigation work like Stanzer, or working with Harry and Guber. And wouldn't the Fae migrating to Neighborlee be surprised when they learned what had happened to him? Not that he was in any hurry to tell them, because he just didn't want to have to deal with the sympathy right now.

If he could stay here in Neighborlee, that would suit him just fine.

Stay in Neighborlee and marry Holly.

Maurice took one last look at the ring tucked safely in its crystal box, swallowed hard, and put it down deep inside the pocket of his jeans.

Yeah, he was going to marry Holly. That meant he had to find a real job. No way was he going to be like some bums among the Fae, who got themselves into trouble and had to flee the Fae realms. They were so predictable, resorting to finding gullible princesses or shepherdesses to trick into marrying them, so they could claim diplomatic asylum and live the good life for thirty or forty years, until things cooled down back home. He was here for the long haul.

He strolled down the streets, not really with any plan in mind. Eventually, he would end up at the library and surprise Holly and walk her home from work. It was about time he started looking outward and thinking about her, looking after her, going to her instead of making her come running to him.

Maurice smiled a little wider, recalling how she had appeared so quickly yesterday morning, terrified for him. Definitely, Holly had some innate magic of her own, to know what had happened. Angela had confirmed that it wasn't just Holly's link to the shop through the passkey. A bond had formed between her and Maurice and let her know when he was endangered.

It was a little ironic, he realized now, that Holly might just have more magic than him, when it was his magical heritage that threatened to create the biggest obstacles to a future together. But that was okay. As long as they could be together, the other little details didn't matter.

Except for the detail of finding a job. Exactly how was he going to get one, when he didn't have all that boring Human paperwork, like a Social Security number and a resume?

The answer came almost as soon as he thought of that question. Maurice looked down the street and saw the sign for the *Neighborlee Tattler*. Not that he wanted to work at the newspaper, but the best place to start finding an answer was to ask a friend. He kind of liked the idea of shocking Lanie Zephyr by showing up, full-size, sans wings.

No one knew yet what had happened to him. Angela had fielded numerous calls throughout the day yesterday from friends calling to ask about the ripples of power and odd dissonances they had felt coming from Divine's. To each one, she promised an explanation much later, and simply said the emergency had passed. At the time, Maurice had been puzzled why she wouldn't just share the news. Then, when his headache cleared up, he appreciated Angela's consideration in letting him break the news of the drastic change in his life in the setting and timing of his choice.

He wondered now how long it would take for Lanie to recognize him. As he crossed the parking lot to the newspaper building, Maurice nearly laughed aloud to realize that his head had lost the last tingling remnant of that scorched feeling and his skin didn't prickle under the touch of the sun. Nothing like getting his mind on something besides feeling sorry for himself, to finish his recovery. He strolled through the front door, which was propped open.

"Can I help you?" the skinny, red-haired woman at the front desk asked.

"Is Lanie here?" He looked around, struck yet again by how different familiar places looked when he wasn't five inches tall and flying through. Perspective was everything.

"Somebody taking my name in vain?" Lanie called.

Maurice turned to the left and saw the ramp leading up to the next level of the office. The *Neighborlee Tattler* had taken over and annexed the buildings on either side as it had grown through the decades. Where floors weren't even from one building to another, ramps were installed. That was convenient for Lanie in her wheelchair. She turned a corner, slid down the ramp to the main floor, and skidded to a stop. Her mouth dropped open as her head tilted back and she looked him over, head to foot and back again.

"What kind of trouble are you in now?" she finally said, after several crackling seconds of silence. Then she burst out laughing and opened her arms. "I felt something happen over at Divine's, but I never guessed it was you. This has got to be a great story."

"That's an understatement." Maurice bent to hug Lanie.

"That's the hug I owe you from last summer," she said as she released him and he stood up. "Hey, Casey, we're going out for some air. If Conrad starts looking for me, tell him I'll be back in maybe...what, fifteen minutes? Half an hour?" She looked up at Maurice.

"Depends. I haven't told the story yet, so I don't know how long it'll take."

"Uh huh. I'll let you know if I'm coming back at all." She winked at the woman at the front desk and headed for the door.

Lanie led the way through the door, down the ramp and across the parking lot in silence.

"So, did you break the curse, or did you get out early for good behavior?" she asked, once they had crossed the street and headed down the sidewalk in the general direction of the center of town. "That was the sonic boom I felt yesterday?"

"Got caught between Angela and someone trying to yank her into a really mean painting."

"Sounds painful."

"It was." He exhaled sharply, trembling for a moment as the

memory of all those sensations washed over him again. By the time they reached the shade of the gazebo in the town center, he had given her the general details. He didn't have to fill in any details on Ethan, because Lanie was completely up-to-date on that part of the story. She winced and hissed and shook her head in all the appropriate places. Once, she reached out to squeeze his hand.

"So, what are you planning on doing? If you're here for the long haul, I mean." Lanie went in reverse, putting her back to the wall of the gazebo, next to the end of the bench that circled the inside of the shelter.

"I'm here for the long haul, whether I get my magic back or not." He settled down next to her and laughed a little when his legs ached. "I'm not used to going around under my own power," he explained, when Lanie gave him a questioning frown. "What I want to do is find a job and marry Holly. Seems like that's the responsible, logical order. Not that I want to wait to marry her." He pulled the crystal box out of his pocket as he spoke and handed it to Lanie.

"Whoa. That is serious." She whistled as she opened the box and got a good look at the ring. "And really romantic," she added, after he told her about the dream when Holly found the ring. She grinned as she handed the ring back to him and patted his arm. "I'm glad for you. But finding a job... Well, you might just have come to the right place."

"What? Delivering papers?"

"That's a kid's job. You can't make a living delivering papers two days a week. No, I'm thinking about all the paperwork, getting you a legal identity, proving you're not an illegal alien."

"I am, if you think about it."

"Yeah, well, the jury's still out on whether the Lost Kids are from another planet and we're illegal aliens, too." Lanie scooted around in her chair as if getting more comfortable. "The Sheridans have connections. They've gotten really good at helping people in trouble start entirely new lives."

"You're serious?" Maurice rolled the crystal box around between his palms, feeling his pulse speed up and his breathing get fast and shallow as relief and anticipation rolled through him in competing waves.

"Sure," Lanie said. "But what do other Fae do when they settle on Earth? Do they just use their magic to conjure up fake I.D., and use their magic to alter the records and such?"

"I don't know. The thing is, it's not really an issue, because they have magic to distract people who ask the wrong questions, and they can just pop out if things get sticky. Or just do the old, 'Those aren't the droids you're looking for,' routine. I could ask Lori and Alexi and the others, I suppose, but..." He shook his head. Suddenly, there was too much to think about. Things were easier when he had no idea if any of his goals were possible. "How much time can you give me right now?"

"Why?"

"I might need you to run interference for me." He got up and headed for the ramp down from the gazebo. Lanie followed him with a mental shove to get her wheelchair speeding along. "I didn't lose everything." He gestured at her wheelchair as she rolled along next to him without any deceleration. "I can feel when you use your power."

"That's a good sign. You'll get something back." She turned her chair at the intersection of paths through the town center. "Or maybe you don't want to get your magic back?"

"Depends on what Holly says."

"Uh huh. That's what I thought." From Lanie's grin, Maurice knew she approved.

He expected to start getting scared, the closer they got to the library building, but all he felt was that glorious, hold-your-breath pressured feeling he got when the clock ticked closer to midnight on his day of partial freedom. *Worth the price,* he thought again, and nearly tripped on the uneven flagstones of the path leading up to the library.

"Just don't do that going down the aisle," Lanie said, and detoured to the right, where the ramp to get up on the library porch was hidden behind some bushes.

Chapter Eleven

Maurice waited for her to catch up with him, and then held the door open. She gave him a regal nod of thanks, her expression somber. Then ruined it by sticking her tongue out at him as soon as he stepped through the door and caught up with her. He muffled his laughter and looked around the big main room of the converted old house. He had no idea where Holly was right this moment and felt his first flicker of regret at the loss of his magic. It used to be, he knew exactly where she was, even from all the way on the other side of town.

But wait ...

Maurice caught his breath at a faint tickling awareness on his right. He followed the sensation, through two archways, into the craft room. Holly sat in the window seat, reading aloud a story about a poetic mouse, while a gaggle of six-year-olds sat at half-height tables and made their own mice out of gray cotton balls and strings and pipe cleaners. He waited in the doorway, Lanie silent beside him, until Holly read the last word and closed her book.

"Well?" she said, looking around at the children. "Do you think you could do what--" Holly stopped short, her gaze locking with his. For a moment she was utterly still, eyes wide, and Maurice's heart stuttered in panic. The same panic he felt whenever Holly came into the shop and didn't see him right away, and he was sure the Disciplinary Council's mercy had ended and he was again invisible and inaudible to her.

Holly smiled and put the book aside on the window seat. Maurice hurried across the room, weaving between the little tables, before she could stand up and he lost his nerve. He fumbled the crystal box from his pocket as he nearly slid to a stop on one knee in front of her.

"Maurice!" Holly squeaked, as he opened the box and held it out to her on his flattened palm. Her eyes got even wider. "Where did you find it?"

"At Divine's, of course." His panic washed away at this sign she remembered that especially enchanting dream adventure they had shared. "I love you, Holly Berry. Marry me?"

"You silly man," she whispered, tears in her eyes, which sparkled and crinkled up with laughter. "You've asked me a dozen times already."

"Yeah, but those were dreams. This time it's real."

"Well, I've got news for you. All those times were real for me."

"Then--" He choked, feeling as if his heart would thud its way out his chest. "Then the answer stays the same?"

When she nodded, he whooped and scooped her up in his arms and spun her around, surrounded by the chatter and questions and cheers of the story time children.

~~~~~

Ethan knew better than to keep the talisman with him. If the Von Helados were as powerful as he feared, they would find it no matter where he hid it in his office or apartment. He took his time driving back home from Neighborlee, thinking hard, discarding one option after another. His first impulse was to bury it, but the only park available to him wasn't particularly large. It wouldn't take much searching to find the spot that looked like it had been recently disturbed and dug up.

He drove five hours away from Neighborlee and perpendicular to his straight route home, stopped at a post office, and mailed the talisman to his friend at the testing laboratory. He asked him to check if anything about the talisman had changed since the first round of tests, and to send the report to him by mail rather than email or by phone. Then five days later, send the talisman back to him. If the Von Helados wanted to go on a wild goose chase, trying to track down the package through the U.S. Postal Service, he wished them luck.

Of course, he meant bad luck.

The delay would help, even if those black-clad errand-runners did get hold of the talisman in the end. It would be a longer delay than if they had to go to the park and dig for it. Besides, he was pretty sure the local cops or park attendants wouldn't be very happy to have him digging there in the first place. He couldn't do it in broad daylight, and he knew better than to take that talisman out at night. Something told him that while moonlight might be friendly, darkness would work against him.
~~~~~

Maybe later, when things calmed down and everything was settled, he would laugh at himself for suddenly believing down in his bones in the very things he had denied for so long. As it was, those colorful sparkles and whispers of laughter had returned to the edges of his awareness. If they didn't get too loud or active, he supposed he could put up with them.

When the Von Helados appeared in his office, the afternoon after he got back from his trip to Neighborlee, two days after Maurice turned from an oversized dragonfly into a full-size man, Ethan was grateful for the company of those sparkles. Even if the dark cloud he sensed surrounding the Von Helados manifested into reality and snuffed out the lights in his office, he was sure the sparkles would surround him with light.

No more darkness, he vowed. No more fighting not to see and hear. No matter how illogical something was, he would embrace otherness. The only other choice was to dry up until he was nothing but whispering sand, and insanity.

"We are ready to go to Neighborlee to take custody of our dear Annabelle," Mrs. Von Helado announced. Her voice sounded rich with satisfaction, which just made the hairs stand up on Ethan's arms and the back of his neck. "I assumed, when I did not hear from you, that there was no reaction, she did not recognize the coin when you encountered her?"

"Nope. Sorry. She was really nice the first time I saw her, but then the last two times … yeah, I can believe she needs someone looking after her. It was like she was scared of the whole world."

"Ah, so sad." The old woman shook her head, her mouth flattening in disappointment, but not before it twitched in a smirk Ethan wanted to smack off her face.

The nasty old bat thinks Angela's damaged, even if she didn't touch the talisman. She's gonna get a nasty surprise when she shows up in town, isn't she? Hopefully she can't get into town.

"I would like the coin back. Perhaps seeing it in conjunction with a familiar face will help trigger a return of her memories." She sat back in her chair and one of her silent flunkies stepped up next to her and held out a black-gloved hand. Who wore black leather gloves in the daytime in the heat of early summer, anyways?

Maybe they didn't want to touch the talisman with their bare flesh, either?

"Yeah, makes sense." Ethan made to pull his drawer open, then stopped. "Sorry. Completely forgot. I put it in my safety deposit box, for safekeeping. Can't be too careful about something like that."

"Indeed not." That smirk caught up one corner of her mouth.

"By the time we can get there, the bank'll be closed," he said, gesturing at the clock on the wall, which read 4:45. "If you want, we can meet there first thing in the morning, and I'll go in and get it and hand it over."

That suited Mrs. Von Helado, so they arranged the time and place. Ethan didn't like how pleasant and understanding she was. How could the old woman not know something had happened in Neighborlee? Did she feel nothing but a weakening of the shield surrounding the town, as Angela theorized? Why didn't she feel when the talisman tried to yank Maurice through the painting? How could she accept the flimsy story Ethan had given her?

If he had been alone, he might have stopped right there and banged his head on his desk for thinking such things.

If he hadn't already made the choice to fully embrace the otherness that seemed determined to saturate his life.

Maybe he really was insane, thinking as if the otherness was aware, able to think and choose and act on its own? And not only aware, but aware of him, in particular?

Ethan promised himself he would discuss all his speculations and ideas with Angela. She would explain so everything made sense. When things had settled down again. If they ever did.

Somehow, that made everything all right, inside his head and his gut. Choosing to accept the otherness gave him two more choices. Either ally with the Von Helados and their evident power and threat, or ally with Angela and Divine's Emporium and all the weirdness woven through the air and soil of Neighborlee.

"No-brainer," Ethan whispered, after the Von Helados left.

Just like before, he presented an outward appearance of normality, keeping to his usual routine. He waited until his regular office hours were over, neatened up for a prolonged absence, left messages with people who would look after his mail and answering machine and apartment, and went home to pack for another journey to Neighborlee. This time, Ethan suspected it wouldn't be a fast, in-and-out visit.

Maybe he should consider moving to Neighborlee? Would Stanzer welcome a partner in the business? Ethan grinned at himself in the mirror over his dresser as he contemplated the idea. He liked it more the longer he thought about it.

What had changed him so much, so drastically, in such a short time?

He suspected the answer had long golden and strawberry-tinted hair and blue eyes, and guarded mysteries and wonders that could drive a man insane.

At nightfall, he got in his car and headed out of town. The multi-colored sparkles settled around him, inside and outside his car, coating his shoulders, resting on his dashboard. Ethan didn't know why, but they were clearer, more distinct, as if his vision had changed and he had been unable to focus until now.

"Okay, kids," he muttered as he left the city limits and the Interstate on-ramp lay before him. "If you could be on the lookout for trouble, let me know if the Von Helados get on my tail, I'd be much obliged."

A whisper of something that sounded like laughter tickled his ears, and for the first time in what felt like decades, it didn't bother him. Maybe in a while, he'd grow to like it.

Ethan turned on the radio as night settled around him. He didn't pay attention until the news came on at 10pm, announcing a break-in at his bank back home.

"Couldn't wait for morning, could you?" he muttered, and reached for his cell phone.

Stanzer answered his phone on the fourth ring. He didn't ask any questions when Ethan related the Von Helados' visit, the lie about the talisman, and the bank break-in. There was no telling what those people would do now that they knew there was no talisman in the bank, and Ethan didn't even have a safety deposit box. Would they waste time tracking down the talisman, or head straight to Neighborlee?

Ethan hoped with all his might they would take the first choice. He hoped they needed the talisman to do anything at all to Angela. And that his tactic had bought them enough time to prepare for battle.

"I'll call Angela and warn her right now," Stanzer said. "How far are you from here?"

"Three hours if I risk a ticket. Hey, do you see the sparkly things that float around Angela and sound like kids laughing?"

"Sometimes. Why?"

"What are they called?"

"Winkies. They're more a nuisance than anything, but Angela considers them friends. Why?"

"They seem to like me. I hope that's a good sign."

"For us, definitely." Stanzer sighed. "I have to confess, we weren't quite sure what to make of you. The readings Lanie got were sort of mixed. And especially after what happened with Maurice."

"Is he okay? Angela wouldn't let me stay around and see how things turned out."

"He's fine. Pretty happy about it, actually. When all this is cleared up with the Von Helados, I promise, you'll get the whole story."

"Promise me something else?"

"Depends."

Ethan grinned into the highway darkness ahead of him. "Think about maybe taking on a business partner?"

"Sounds interesting."

It sounded good to the winkies, if Ethan could judge the atmosphere in the car after he put down his cell phone. He could have sworn they were singing. What they were singing, he couldn't begin to guess.

~~~~~

Angela looked out at the moonlight filling the park below her home like water filling a misty lake. She laughed at herself, keeping watch for Maurice to come home. Holly had called after she got off work to report that she and Maurice were going for a long picnic. Ordinarily, Angela wouldn't be worried about him. On his days free of his punishment, there were plenty of magical forces to keep watch over Maurice, and usually plenty of friends with gifts. Ordinarily, he was too busy concentrating on Holly to get into trouble. Things weren't ordinary anymore, however. Ordinary for Divine's Emporium, of course, not for the mundane world outside the borders of Neighborlee.

Maurice had shown some magical sensitivity when he saw the ring that had been conjured by Holly's dream. He had seen the
~~~~~

window into what Angela considered a "playground world." He did have all his magical awareness. But was it enough to help him avoid trouble?

More important, did he have enough magical sensitivity to make him a target for danger? Usually, the people in Neighborlee who ran into strange and unusual things were safe, because they didn't see, didn't hear, didn't feel the parallel dimensions and doorways to otherness that were only a breath away from them. Some strange law of magical physics Angela had never pursued or analyzed made them invisible to things that were invisible to them, untouchable by things they couldn't touch. Most of the time.

The residents of the town who could sense and do and understand the amazing and unusual were the ones who ran into trouble. They became targets of the good and evil forces from beyond Human understanding and experience.

So just where did Maurice stand in that scale of comprehension and danger?

"Guard him," she whispered to the winkies who churned around her in ever-thickening clouds.

Perhaps a quarter of them streaked off to do her bidding. The majority stayed with her.

That frightened her.

The winkies weren't creatures of reason. They could be guided by force of will, by emotions, and their own instinct, their sense of good and evil, laughter and love and danger. So why did they stay by her?

The ringing of her phone startled a gasp out of her. Angela turned and looked across her tiny living room and glared at the phone. It didn't shut up. Sighing loudly, she crossed the room, half-hoping whoever was calling would give up. Probably tomorrow morning, a friend or customer would come in and scold her once again that they had only wanted to leave a message, not intrude on her personal time, and she needed to get an answering machine.

Angela let her lips relax into an approximation of a smile as she thought of her usual response: The fewer machines inside Divine's Emporium, the better. Even something as simple as an answering machine. If she really wanted something set up to take messages when she didn't feel like answering the phone, she would ask one of her Fae friends to set a spell. Then power outages and dead batteries would never bother her. Even better, she could screen calls and even have separate messages to deal with different callers, such as telling salesmen and pollsters and political fundraisers not to call back.

The amusement that came with that thought died when she heard Stanzer's voice, even before his words made any sense.

"Do you want me to come by, wait with you?" he asked, after he passed on what Ethan had told him and the estimate for when he would show up at Divine's Emporium.

"He's coming as a friend. And Maurice should be back soon." Angela flinched, catching herself thinking of Maurice as having wings and magic. Those days were gone.

"Not just me," he said. "The entire Hunt. And if there's trouble, the Hounds will show up for you, Angela."

"Have you ever considered that the Hounds might be blocked from being involved with certain kinds of magical...situations?"

"Yeah." He sighed, sounding just as weary as she felt. "But we won't know what their limits are until we try, right?"

"True." Angela finally sat down. She had been pleased that Serena was staying the summer with Dawn and Cinden in Dawn's apartment in Stanzer's building. The girl was her ward, and was supposed to be living with her, but that wouldn't officially start until the school year began, just for the sake of the child welfare authorities. She didn't want the Hunt to be involved in this, even though she knew they had gifts and experience that effectively negated their chronological age and the label of "children." Legally, most of them were minors. Spiritually and in all other ways, they were seasoned warriors.

"I know what you're thinking," Stanzer said when the silence stretched out between them.

"Really?" She decided to be amused.

"You're the town's guardian and you won't let anybody face the fire for you. Not even the people who owe you, who love you."

"Oh, now that's a low blow. How dare you use the love card?" A few bubbles of laughter escaped her.

"Angela..."

"Oh, very well. Come out in the chill and mist and risk a silly cold. I'll just dose all of you with something loathsome and you'll feel like idiots, staying up late for no good reason."

"What are you talking about?" His voice had a catch in it.

Angela stood and picked up the phone, walking to the window as far as the long extension cord would allow her. The mist from the park had crept up the slope and surrounded her house in moonlit white as far as she could see. Droplets had even begun to condense on her window.

"The mist," she said. "It's cold outside, and there's a mist crawling up from the park. You can see the air currents swirling it around."

"It's a scorching night. You'd swear it was August. Everybody is camped out in Dawn's place because it's wide open and has the best air conditioning. And the air isn't moving, otherwise they'd be up on the roof to take advantage of the breezes. Angela--"

"It's already started." She silently cursed herself for a fool, letting her worries for Maurice distract her from what should have been patently obvious. The Von Helados had to believe she had been damaged or at least weakened by the attack of the talisman and had begun their next attack. If she was lucky, they were wasting time looking for Ethan and didn't realize he was already on his way to Neighborlee.

"We're on our way."

"No, John, don't--" Angela stood a moment, listening to the dial tone. Maybe tomorrow, if there was a tomorrow, she would be upset or amused, or both, that Stanzer had hung up on her.

She suspected that even with the help of the Hounds, the Hunt wouldn't be able to get into Divine's Emporium. If the mist was what she feared, they wouldn't even be able to find her home.

The question now, she supposed, was exactly what the telephone connection said about the magical reach and strength and skill of her enemies. Did mechanical, electrical, modern things have the ability to overpower that magic? Or was their power not quite as encompassing as they needed it to be, to cut her off from friends and allies and help? Or had they allowed the telephone to work to taunt her? To fool her into thinking she wasn't cut off from the rest of the world?

"Can any of you leave?" she whispered to the winkies, and closed her eyes, concentrating on an image of them flying away, finding Maurice, warning him. They swirled around her in a thickening cloud, coating her in a shimmering layer of ever-shifting colors. Just when she felt a flicker of exasperation and a glimmer of fear that she had lost the ability to communicate with them, several layers of that cloud swirled away and through the wall, to the outside.

Angela wrapped her arms around herself, staring at the wall they had gone through, willing them to stay away and not return. Returning would mean they hadn't been able to get out, pierce the barrier she sensed enveloping the shop. Her heart thundered in her ears and her lungs burned, and she gasped, exhaling abruptly and then inhaling, and laughed at herself. She had actually been holding her breath as she waited.

The seconds turned to minutes. Downstairs the ornate, gold-trimmed clock that sat in the front window chimed eleven. She waited, sending her awareness down to the foundations of the shop, through the walls, testing the protective net, feeling for the first sneaky, slithering attack, whether it was a grain of sand or a whisper in the darkness trying to penetrate her soul.

The flute clock, as Maurice had called it, slipped out of its dimensional slit and tweetled the quarter hour.

Enough of waiting. Angela got up and went downstairs.

The phone behind the counter rang just as she reached the main room. She glanced out the windows on the street in front of Divine's Emporium. There was nothing but swirling white mist.

"Angela, are you okay?" Stanzer asked. Static rose up in a wave and she waited before answering.

"I'm fine, but I'm guessing you either can't get through the mist, or you can't find the shop at all."

"These guys play hardball. Listen, we're going to try to call the Hounds. Maybe they can penetrate that mist. Bring you out."

"No. If, as you say, they've put me under their guardianship, don't you think they would have appeared by now if I was in any danger?"

Silence for a few seconds. Angela had such a clear image of him scowling at his cell phone, biting his lip, she almost had to laugh. Almost. The darkness of her own shop suddenly felt wrong, and she reached for the light switch before she frightened herself.

"I really hate it when you do that," Stanzer muttered.

"Do what?"

"Refuse to be the damsel in distress."

"John." Laughter bubbled out of her, pushing the shadows back into the walls where they had seeped through, easing the chill out of her bones, and making her aware that she had indeed grown chilled. "I haven't been a damsel in distress in... Well, in such a long time, I've quite forgotten how to be one." Angela caught her breath as her dream of the garden of moonlight and shadows filled her mind, to the point that it threatened to overwhelm the warmth and comfort of the shop room around her.

"Well, learn how. I'm going to contact Lanie and her gang, see what they can figure out to do. Between all the illegal aliens in this town, we can gang up on the magic that's picking on you."

"As long as you all stay out of that mist. And do me a favor? Talk to others in town, those who are still awake at this hour. Find out what they see. I'd wager that those who aren't magic-sensitive see nothing wrong at all. Only those with any chance of impacting the outcome of tonight's battle are affected by this mist."

"That's kind of powerful magic," he said quietly.

"Old, experienced magic that has learned to focus, identify the threats, and not waste energy defending on every front when opposition only comes from one place."

After Stanzer hung up, Angela turned on every light in the shop, then the stairway landing lights, then the lights in the storage rooms. She spent some time in the painting room, arranging the most dangerous paintings so they faced each other. If the protective spells and barriers failed, the nasty things waiting to break free would simply leap into another world inhabited by creatures just as nasty as they were, rather than invading Earth.

At least, that was the theory. Angela hoped the attack was on her, personally, and not the shop itself, in an attempt to shatter dimensional doorways, allowing nightmares loose into unsuspecting worlds. Most especially not her world, her town that she had guarded and loved for decades.

On the way down the stairs again, she paused on the second-floor landing and stared long at the image of the stone walls and silver gates slowly rippling in and out of focus through the wallpaper. Was it trying to come into being tonight? Or was it finally fading away? What would happen if she touched the latch of the silver gate of her own free will, pushed it open, and stepped into the garden of moonlight and mist and shadows beyond it?

No. Now was not the time to go through those gates. A battle waited, and she wouldn't leave her friends to fight it for her.

Angela hurried down the stairs. The winkies swirled around her, suddenly agitated. She paused, frustrated by the sudden volume of her heart's thuds, drowning out all other sounds. She took deep breaths, willing herself to calm, and heard the distinct sound of a car door opening in front of the shop.

What amplified the sound? Her own nervousness, or the mist?

She was at the front door almost before she knew what she wanted to do. The winkies' lights dimmed, all of them turning to a pale green, before shifting to a nearly navy blue. They didn't flee her, and Angela took that as an encouraging sign. The car door outside slammed shut, and she opened the door to look out. Just to look out. She knew better than to go past the threshold.

Ethan stood on the curb, staring up at the house as the mist billowed out to surround his car, enclosing him in the whiteness.

"It wants him here, doesn't it?" Angela whispered. The winkies shimmered into pink for a moment, and then their lights dimmed more.

"They're coming," Ethan called. "This isn't normal, is it?" He spread his arms, taking in the mist that enclosed them in a dim, silver-gray-white world. At his movements, winkies flared to life, red and purple, clinging to his clothes and streaking his hair. He scowled and flicked a bright green point of light off the tip of his nose.

Angela laughed. She couldn't help it.

At the sound of her voice, all the winkies coating her and Ethan shimmered with more light, their colors shifting to pinks and greens and bright blues.

"You can see them now, can't you?" she called.

"Yeah, and it's driving me nuts!" But he grinned at her, uncertainly, like someone who didn't have much practice in smiling. "Look, those lunatics who hired me broke into my bank, looking for that cursed coin that hurt your friend. Even if they don't find it, I've got the feeling they're on their way here to finish the job."

"A job that never got started," she reminded him.

"Yeah, true, but won't you be safer getting out of town? Lead them on a wild goose chase?" He gestured back at his car. "Let me protect you. I know I'm not the dragon-slaying knight that chick in the wheelchair thought she saw, but... Heck, maybe I can figure out how."

Angela caught her breath, when a trick of the shifting darkness and pale light and the changing glow of the winkies suddenly wrapped him in dark silver armor. Ethan's blue eyes were the scowling eyes of her silent stone knight from the garden of her dreams.

"Let's get out of here, Angela. I swear, whatever it takes, I'll do it to protect you."

"No. I can't leave." She swallowed hard at the sudden thrill of panic that wrapped around her throat. "And you have to get inside. Now. Before the mist gets any thicker."

She gestured at the winkies coating him. Their light had faded again as the mist crept closer around him. If their light went out...

"Ethan, come inside now. You're only safe--we're only safe--inside the walls here."

She saw the struggle of mind and soul in his face, the stiffness of his posture. He wanted to believe. He didn't want to believe.

A thick tendril of mist looked like a hand, rising up to wrap around his face, around his throat. Angela saw the moment Ethan's gaze shifted and he saw what she saw. He ducked and dodged and tugged aside his jacket, revealing the shoulder holster and the handgun that gleamed like a sword in moonlight. Mortal weapons were useless here. What tragedy would have to befall him before he learned that painful lesson?

"Okay," he called, not yet drawing the weapon, and pivoting with every other step to look around himself as he approached the wrought iron gate. "I'm coming in."

The gate refused to swing open when he pushed on it.

If the enemies wanted him here, letting him through the mist to reach her house, why wouldn't they let him get to the house?

Unless their whole purpose was just what Ethan had proposed? For her to leave with him? To get her to leave Divine's Emporium and all the magical safety woven into its physical being.

Angela gripped the doorframe, imagining the mist thrusting a tentacle at her to yank her outside. She watched as Ethan leaned into the gate and pushed, hard, so she could see the bulging of the muscles in his arms through his coat, saw the strain in his face. He growled a curse, put both hands on the stone post the gate was anchored to, and swung himself up and over in one smooth motion.

Gale force winds plunged down from the sky as his feet touched the flagstone path to her door. Ethan stumbled back, nearly impaling his buttocks on the pointed tops of the iron fence posts. Wind blinded him, creating ripples in his skin, pressing his eyelids closed, tossing debris into his eyes and mouth. The winkies were torn away, their lights going out completely.

"Stop it!" Angela shouted, and stepped forward, reaching out to him.

Her winkies shrieked as she put one foot over her threshold. She froze, feeling a force yanking on her leg, a sensation as if something hot and prickly and stinging grabbed hold of her ankle.

"No!" Ethan gasped. Through the assault of the wind on his face, she saw his sudden terror. "Don't come out. That's what they want. You'll die."

Angela sagged back, bracing herself on the doorframe, shivering as she remembered almost too late the dream where the knight had pulled her off the porch of Divine's Emporium and she had shriveled in his arms.

A funnel of blackness spun down from the ceiling of darkening mist, the narrow tip aiming for Ethan.

She shouted his name and pointed.

He flung himself forward to dodge it. The winds resisted him, keeping him nearly upright, but he did gain a few feet. The funnel twisted, following him as he went to his hands and knees, digging into the gaps between the flagstones with his fingers, pulling himself forward.

Angela watched, willing all her strength to him.

That prickling, stinging sensation returned, and she gasped, throwing herself backward as she realized she had edged forward, putting the toes of one foot, her hand, her nose and forehead over the threshold. The enemy wanted to lure her out of the safety of Divine's Emporium, into the mist and darkness and wind. It would keep Ethan away from her, tormenting him, until the tension was too much for her and she forgot herself and raced out to help him.

Chapter Twelve

When this was over, Angela promised herself she would find a way to punish her enemies so they never rose up against her ever again. This was wrong. It was cruel and evil. She rarely used the power at her disposal for her own satisfaction, but she would feel no guilt in using it now.

She dug her fingers into the doorframe, holding herself fast, and watched Ethan struggle.

He had made it halfway up the flagstone path now, his clothes stained with sweat and the debris ground into them. In the flickering light, she saw darkness on his hands and feared he had torn his fingers open in the struggle to pull himself along the stones. The enemy would pay for that, too.

Angela sagged, breathless for a moment as images raced through her mind. Memories, she realized, with a pang that took her breath away.

Ethan standing in a stream, bare-chested, laughing, bronzed by the sun. His trousers rolled up to his knees. His hair long, tangled and curly. Holding out those long-fingered hands to her, beckoning. She gave her hand into his and stepped into the stream, holding her long skirts high. He teased her, waggling his eyebrows at the sight of her legs bared to the knees. When she stepped back, pretending pique, he roared laughter, lunged, and caught her up, to throw her over his shoulder and stride across the stream. She kicked and wriggled and laughed and he swatted her behind before setting her down on the other side with a thump.

And captured her mouth in a kiss that went on forever.

"No!" Ethan shouted, tearing Angela out of the memories. "Go back!"

Gasping, she flung herself backward, falling down hard in the doorway of the shop. She had stepped forward as if to cross that stream from her memory. To go to him. And nearly left the shop entirely. Her legs stung up to the knees and her fingers felt nearly numb and the skin of her face felt as if it had been scoured by the debris and force of the wind. Angela scrambled backward, putting two more feet of space between her feet and the threshold.

She ached, fighting tears of fury and a deep longing as familiar as her own breath. Yet it had no part of the life she had made for herself in Neighborlee. Had she once felt that pain as if she had been torn into two pieces, as if everything inside her had been emptied out and scoured clean? Had it been so long that the scar had gone numb, or she had forgotten?

Or was this another trick of the enemy, trying to make her believe Ethan was her lost love, her knight from the midnight garden? Did they try to awaken loneliness she had never known before, to trick her into going out into that storm?

"Angela?" Maurice's shout drew her back to the doorway.

Holly and Maurice came around the side of the house. They had probably come up from the park into the back yard. The mist swirled away from them and glimmers of the moonlight outside the enchantment shone through, reaching down the tunnel their presence had created. Angela struggled to her feet, leaning against the doorframe, trying to wrap her mind around the multiple reasons why the enchantment didn't affect Holly and Maurice, yet kept Stanzer and his allies from getting through to her.

"Stay there!" she shouted, listening to a half-formed idea.

Intent, she suspected, was half the battle, and half the solution. Maurice and Holly were merely coming back from a picnic, coming home, with no idea that a magical battle was taking place in the front yard. Their thoughts were elsewhere, focused on each other, in effect shielding them from the enemy's touch and notice. Angela had no idea how long that window of freedom would last, but she intended to use it.

In the back room, she found a coil of rope and a ten-pound disc weight from a used bench press set she had bought but hadn't put out in the shop yet. She tied the weight to the end of the rope, swung it around as far as the doorway would let her, and tossed it to Maurice. Interestingly, the wind didn't affect the weight and rope at all, just like the enchantment didn't affect Maurice and Holly.

Because they weren't interfering with the enemy's plans.

For the moment.

"Give it to him, then get up here," she shouted, as Maurice caught hold of the rope.

It was good to have people around who were accustomed to

strange happenings and trusted her enough not to ask questions. Maurice and Holly linked arms. They both took hold of the rope with their free hands and crossed the yard to where Ethan still inched forward along the flagstone path, with the wind pushing him away. The black funnel cloud continued to jab at him and he rolled from side to side, dodging it.

Angela frowned, suddenly seeing a pattern in those jabs. If she didn't know better, she would think it was trying to hit Ethan's coat pockets. That made no sense.

Since when does evil make sense? Who said it ever had to make sense? someone asked in her memory. She caught her breath when she suspected that laughing, rich male voice was Ethan's. But when had they ever had such a conversation?

On Maurice and Holly's second step, the enchantment swirled around them. Angela grabbed hold of the rope, throwing all her weight against it to keep it taut and help them stay upright. They were farther out in the yard than Ethan, and they let the wind push them. They swung around on the end of the rope so the action brought them against him. Maurice tripped over Ethan, while Holly went to her knees next to him. The wind shrieked, louder and higher, and pulled at their clothes. Ethan struggled to get into a sitting position. Maurice and Holly worked to wrap the rope around him.

"Now let go!" Angela shouted, half-afraid her voice couldn't be heard over the uproar of the wind.

All this time, the attacking funnel cloud had ignored Maurice and Holly, except when their hands got in the way of another seeming attempt to get at Ethan's pocket.

Angela shuddered as an idea came to her. What if the enemy was trying to get something *inside* Divine's Emporium? Was the resistance simply to delay him until they could put something in his pocket, while convincing her they didn't want him to get to her? Angela imagined Ethan finally reaching the shop, battered and exhausted, and her so busy tending to him she wouldn't realize she had let the enemy within her walls until it was too late, and inimical magic had a foothold.

"Very well," she muttered, as Holly and Maurice responded to her gestures and rolled away from Ethan. "Have it your way. Or so you think."

Forewarned was forearmed.

When Holly and Maurice were only a few yards away from Ethan, the enchantment let go of them. The wind no longer pulled at their hair and clothes. The tunnel of moonlight calm caught up with them again. They joined hands and ran up to the porch and inside the shop.

If the enemy really wanted to keep Ethan from getting into the shop, they wouldn't have allowed Holly and Maurice to join her and help her pull him inside.

"You sure this guy is worth it?" Maurice grabbed hold of the rope and leaned backward, helping to pull Ethan to the porch.

Ethan got to his feet again, leaning into the force of the wind, and let the rope guide him. It was as if he were pushing on some huge, invisible object with his shoulder, bracing against the ground and shoving with his feet. Angela watched the funnel cloud as they pulled, bringing Ethan closer to safety a foot at a time. The evil enchanted thing's movements grew quicker, more frantic.

"Gotcha," she muttered, when the cloud slipped its tip into Ethan's left pants pocket, and then pulled back.

It made a few more jabs at him, as Ethan stumbled up onto the porch, but the winds softened and the funnel cloud didn't come anywhere near making contact with him. He took bigger, faster steps as the resistance weakened. Angela shook her head at the foolishness and arrogance of her enemy. Did they really think she wouldn't notice?

Then Ethan was inside. Holly slammed the door shut as Angela, Maurice, and Ethan went to their knees in the entryway of the shop, gasping and sweating, filthy and bruised.

"Holly, get three silk scarves from the display," Angela said, still fighting to get her breath back. She scooted backward, freeing her legs from the weight of Ethan sprawled across her.

"What was that all about?" Maurice demanded. He helped Ethan sit upright, and nodded, grinning, when the other man mouthed, "Thanks."

In that moment as they sat there, recovering, wiping sweat and grit from their faces, Angela hoped Ethan and Maurice could be friends. They had certainly contributed to changing each other's lives in a large way, just in the space of a few days.

"What do you want me to do with these?" Holly asked,

returning.

"Ethan's left pocket. Reach in and take out whatever you find, but don't let it touch you. Use the scarves for protection."

"Uh...okay." Holly shrugged. "Sorry."

"That's okay." Ethan wiped his face again. He leaned against the wall, turning to give her easier access to his pocket. A moment later, he swore when he saw the coin lying in Holly's hand, encased in the scarf. "I swear to you, Angela--"

"They wanted you to bring it in here, and they wanted us to be so busy with the battle to get you inside, we wouldn't realize until too late." She struggled against her wobbly legs to get to her feet,

Ethan hurried to get upright and bent to help her. An entirely pleasant jolt of electricity shot through her at the touch of his big, hard, calloused hand on her elbow.

"Thank you." She blushed when her voice cracked and wavered for a second.

"So what do we do with it?" Maurice demanded. "It's back for round two, and I bet those creeps who sent it aren't too far behind."

"We get it out of Divine's Emporium once and for all." Angela shuddered as the rest of her nebulous plan fell into place. "But we take it where they least expect."

At least, I hope so, she added silently.

"I'll take that," Ethan said, holding out his hand for the talisman. Holly carefully slid it into his grasp, with lots of layers of scarf around it on all sides.

"This way." Angela led him up the stairs.

She considered for a few moments tossing the coin into one of the inimical paintings, but what if that was the plan? What if she chose wrongly, and the talisman held the doorway open so the nightmares captured inside the painting could come out? The first attack that had tried to pull Maurice through the painting and burned out his magic had been to separate her from Divine's Emporium. The best response and defense was to take the talisman beyond the influence and reach of her enemies.

Asmondius' words just a few days ago provided the guidance and assurance she needed. As long as she did what she did by choice, not forced into it, she would be in control and effectively negate her enemy's power.

On the second-floor landing, the massive stone arch coalesced into solidity from out of the lavender sprigged wallpaper. The intricate gate of silver swung open on silent hinges. Angela stumbled to a halt, memories crashing through her. She *knew* the garden beyond those gates. It was part of her.

For a stuttering heartbeat, she doubted her plan.

Take her enemy's magic in there? To the most precious spot in all the multi-worlds?

"Here?" Ethan started past her.

For half a second, she wanted to shout "No!" The panic that choked her convinced her. The enemy's hand was too heavy, once again, giving away what it wanted. And didn't want.

"Yes."

Ethan leaped through and she followed, only a step behind.

When they stepped out from the stone arch, the talisman shattered into dust sharper than diamonds, and scattered to the four winds, shredding everything it touched. Angela didn't even try to shield herself as the world shattered around her like a mirror fractured into ten million pieces as fine as grains of sand.

~~~~~

"Lady? My lady?" A man's sobbing voice broke through the haze of rainbows and chimes and the cool, sweet perfume of roses that fogged all her senses.

Angela blinked and turned her head and wasn't surprised to find herself lying in Ethan's arms. That was where she belonged, where she had longed to be for centuries of lonely moonlit nights.

His name wasn't Ethan, any more than hers was Angela, but those were the names they wore now, and would do quite well.

"My love? Please, speak to me." His voice cracked. "Forgive me."

"Forgive you? For defeating our enemies after all this time?" She sat up and laughter bubbled out of her.

Rainbows dashed in a whirlwind around the garden, painting the flowers ten thousand colors and shades. Fountains came to life and birds burst into song. The winkies danced through the air, leaving streamers of iridescent dust in their trail.

This garden had been her home, so long ago she had no memory of the beginning. She had been guardian and guarded both, innocent and alone and unaware of her solitude. Until he stumbled, half-dead, through the barrier, a knight from a world
~~~~~

filled with wars and blood, hatred and death. She had healed him, body and spirit, and they gave each other their hearts.

He broke sacred vows to stay with her, and that opened a gap wide enough for evil to dig one claw into the shielding magic and tear it to shreds.

The only way they could protect their world was to leave it and each other, and trust to the healing magic of sacrifice.

"How many times have we found each other and lost each other again when our enemy attacked?" Angela blinked back happy tears and reclined in his arms again.

"I don't--" Ethan shook his head. "I could remember if I wanted. But I don't want to. The magic wiped our memories to protect us every time we were torn apart, didn't it?"

"We might have died of despair twenty lifetimes ago if we remembered. Love, was it hard?"

"The worst part was learning not to believe." Ethan bent his head to hide his face in her hair. "I think I killed half my soul when I did that."

"No. It only slept. Enough to trick our enemies into thinking they could use you against me."

"That was a fatal mistake," he growled, and turned her in his arms to kiss her.

"Love was too strong," she whispered against his lips.

Nothing mattered then but making up for the centuries of loneliness and separation.

~~~~~

"Asmondius!" Maurice slapped the Wishing Ball. "Come on, I don't care what time it is there, somebody has to be there. Somebody has to hear me."

"Maurice?" Holly wrapped her arms around him. "It's going to be okay. Don't worry."

"Don't worry? Angela's gone!" He twisted free of her arms, though Holly's embrace, her calmness and reasonableness were all that had gotten him through this very long, strange night.

The enchantment separating Divine's Emporium from the rest of Neighborlee had broken with a sonic boom that made the walls ripple and knocked the wind chimes off their hooks to the floor. Every winkie in the entire town had vanished, and that worried Maurice more than he liked to admit. The guardians and every Fae
~~~~~

in Neighborlee had come running.

The gate and wall hidden in the wallpaper on the second-floor landing now stood out in bas relief. The scent of the garden seeped through the air, with the soft sighing of a gentle breeze through the leaves. The faint reverberations of a dimensional doorway that had just closed lingered in the shop. No one could get that doorway to open, no matter what power they threw at it.

Felicity came and threw her EM bursts at the doorway. Lori called Alexi and Guber and Harry, and they combined their magic, to no avail. Maurice was worried when Alexi with his Eclipse-level magic couldn't budge anything.

All the members of the Hunt came together and begged the Hounds to come and help them, but their guardian beasts either weren't listening, or they weren't willing to get involved.

Or, as Holly pointed out with her calm reasonableness, the Hounds knew everything would be all right eventually, and they didn't want to waste their time and energy. Maurice couldn't decide whether to kiss her or shake her.

Everyone had gone home to do some research, come up with theories, get some sleep, and agreed to return in the morning to try again. Maurice knew that was only common sense, but he felt like he and Holly had been abandoned.

"How do you know it's permanent?" Holly stopped him when he started pacing again. "Come on. Let's go upstairs and make some breakfast. Angela could be getting hungry about now and come home on her own. We should have a meal ready for her and Ethan."

"I do hope that ring on your sweetheart's finger means you proposed," Asmondius said, as the transportation globe shimmered open. "She's very good for you, lad." He winked at Holly as he appeared. "What seems to be the problem?"

"Can you put the curse back on me?" Maurice blurted, choking on a need to laugh. Half of him couldn't believe what he was asking, but he was getting desperate.

"Put it back?"

"Yeah--shrink me, give me wings--give me some magic--so I can go through that doorway and look for Angela? Or at least make me able to take care of this place while she's gone."

"Angela..." He settled onto the white bistro chair, clasped his hands in his lap, and closed his eyes. "Angela isn't gone."

"Now see? That's why I need my magic back. Heck, slap another two years on me. Whatever it takes, to rescue her. I'm willing to pay any price." He swallowed hard, realizing how that sounded. "Sorry, Holly Berry. I know that's a rotten deal for you--"

"No, that's okay. I'm worried about Angela, too." Holly slipped her hand into his.

"What good am I to anyone? I'm a wreck," Maurice moaned, and wrapped his arms around her. "What do you mean, exactly, that Angela isn't gone?"

"She's still here in the shop." Asmondius smiled benignly. "If you'd calm down enough to listen, you could feel her presence with what's left of your magic--which seems to be healing quite nicely, I might add. You're quite sensitive to magic, even if you can't manipulate it as easily as you once used to do."

"Fat lot of good it does Angela. Where is she?"

"We're right here." Angela came into the room.

A changed Angela. Blushing, glowing, looking positively shy, she leaned into the arm Ethan had wrapped tight around her. He had that smug look Maurice had seen on a lot of men who had suddenly won the hearts of the girls they loved after a long, hard struggle.

"Wow, where have you two been?" Holly breathed, eyes wide.

Maurice's first guess would be the vintage clothing room, but Angela didn't stock those Renaissance-style clothes. She and Ethan were decked out like high nobility, rich colors and sumptuous cloth, jewels and gold chains. Maurice took a sniff, remembering Asmondius' words, that he was sensitive to magic even if he couldn't manipulate it anymore. He sensed the authenticity of their costumes and smelled the rich aroma of a long-sleeping enchantment finally broken, curses that had run their course and promises fulfilled.

"How long have we been gone?" Ethan asked.

"About nine hours--or an eternity," Holly said, tipping her head up to smirk at Maurice.

"That could come in handy." Ethan caught up Angela's free hand and brushed a slow kiss across her knuckles.

Maurice thought his jaw would hit the floor when Angela blushed.

"Handy?" he asked, just to yank his mind away from the image being painted on it. "Where were you?"

"In our garden..." Angela sighed contentedly. "We were there nearly a week before we remembered we had to come back."

"I can see I'm not needed here," Asmondius announced. "One of these days, you do need to fill in all the missing pieces of the story, my dear." He bowed to Angela as the transportation globe shimmered into being behind him again.

"Asmondius? Do us a favor and post our wedding banns anywhere you think it might matter?" Angela chuckled when the old Fae official stopped short, his mouth dropping open.

Epilogue

Three weeks later...

"You think they're just licking their wounds?" Stanzer said, settling down at his desk in his reorganized office.

"I hope so." Ethan chuckled when his new partner frowned, shaking his head. "You don't know what it's like, living a fraction of a life, with most of who you are locked away behind protective walls so you don't go insane. Knowing there's someone out there who belongs to you, but you can't find her, you don't know where to look or even where to start."

"Uh, yeah." He pointed upward.

It took a moment for Ethan to realize the other man indicated the apartments above them, and one of the occupants.

He instantly felt ashamed. How could he have forgotten the problem Stanzer and Dawn faced? She would soon be a legal adult, but that didn't make it any easier for her and Stanzer to fulfill the betrothal of their childhood, when there was twelve years in age between them. Ethan supposed in some ways, the loss of memories he had endured had made it easier for him to live the centuries away from Angela.

"Sorry," he said. "Feeling sorry for myself again."

"Understandable. You want to rip the hide off those guys and keep ripping it."

"Part of me hopes they are the enemies who separated us. So I can keep punishing them. That they keep trying to come after us." He leaned back in his chair and slowly put one foot, then the other, up on his new, temporarily clean desk. "And part of me hopes that it's just another manifestation of Big Ugly downstairs."

Ethan rather liked the appellation for the dimensional enemy that threatened the safety and balance of Neighborlee.

Whoever they really were, the Von Helados had entirely vanished. Three weeks of searching, of pulling all the strings he could, using all the favors that people in high places owed him, had yielded not a clue, not even a confirmation that the Von Helados had ever existed. They hadn't permanently vanished. Ethan and Angela knew their enemies would return, with a new trick, a new attempt to hurt them. Perhaps to separate them again. Perhaps to take over Divine's Emporium, and control all the wonders and magic the shop guarded.

For now, though, Ethan was at peace.

No, not at peace--happy to the point of being drunken giddy.

Just this morning, the sign painters had finished putting the name of the new partnership on the front window of the storefront office of Stanzer and Jarrod Investigations.

Every afternoon, Ethan went home to Divine's Emporium and to Angela, his bride. The shop had worked its usual dimensional magic without even being asked, expanding her quarters to an almost palatial apartment. Angela had altered her business hours, opening later in the morning and closing earlier in the evening. They enjoyed long, quiet, private hours in the garden behind the shop, or walking in the parkland at the base of the hill. And once a week, they allowed themselves the indulgence of vanishing through the gate into their private garden.

Best of all, every morning, Ethan woke with Angela in his arms. Though it always gave him a pang to release her, he knew it was only for a few hours, not for centuries.

"Hey, guys, how's it going?" Maurice called as he strolled into the office.

"Uh oh," Stanzer said, glancing sideways at Ethan. "Somebody looks pretty happy."

"I got a job!" He struck a pose, chest out, thumbs hooked through nonexistent suspender straps. And the next moment released it when they called out their congratulations. "You're now looking at the official relocation officer for all Fae choosing to live in the northern hemisphere of Earth, as well as the customs inspector for all legal importation of chocolate to the Fae realms."

"Customs inspector for chocolate?" Stanzer and Ethan exchanged grins and shook their heads.

"Big brouhaha went down for months, back home, thanks to finding out that carob is poison for Fae. Lots of legislation going through, calling for inspections and health certifications. It means I'm gainfully employed. Won't be sponging off my Holly."

"Does that mean she'll make an honest man of you at last?" Ethan asked. He chuckled when Maurice went dark red, with hints of purple in his ear tips and a faint hissing of deep blue sparks coming out of his ears. "I guess it does."

"Yeah, and if you guys had shown any patience at all, we could be making it a double wedding," he shot back.

"When it comes to love, and especially when it comes to Angela..." he sighed contentedly, "patience is overrated."

END

Neighborlee, Ohio

(Title, Original Title, Release Date)

Confessions of a Lost Kid (Growing Up Neighborlee) 05/20
Semi-Pseudo-Superheroes (Dorm Rats) 07/20
Virtually London (London Holiday) 09/20
Living Proof (that no good deed goes unpunished) (Living Proof) 11/20
Night of the Living Proof, 01/21
Quitting the Hero Biz (Hero Blues) 03/21
Bride of the Living Proof, 05/21
Shrunk: The Exile of Maurice (Divine's Emporium) 07/21
Return of the Living Proof, 09/21
Allergic to Mistletoe (Have Yourself a Faerie Little Christmas) 11/21
Dawn of the Living Proof, 01/22
Angela's Knight (Divine Knight) 03/22
The Living Proof Gets the Blues, 05/22

About the Author

On the road to publication, Michelle fell into fandom in college and has 40+ stories in various SF and fantasy universes. She has a bunch of useless degrees in theater, English, film/communication, and writing. Even worse, she has over 100 books and novellas with multiple small presses, in science fiction and fantasy, YA, suspense, women's fiction, and sub-genres of romance.

Her official launch into publishing came with winning first place in the Writers of the Future contest in 1990. She was a finalist in the EPIC Awards competition multiple times, winning with *Lorien* in 2006 and *The Meruk Episodes, I-V,* in 2010, and was a finalist in the Realm Awards competition, in conjunction with the Realm Makers convention.

Her training includes the Institute for Children's Literature; proofreading at an advertising agency; and working at a community newspaper. She is a tea snob and freelance edits for a living (MichelleLevigne@gmail.com for info/rates), but only enough to give her time to write. Her newest crime against the literary world is to be co-managing editor at Mt. Zion Ridge Press and launching the publishing co-op, Ye Olde Dragon Books. Be afraid … be very afraid.

www.Mlevigne.com
www.MichelleLevigne.blogspot.com
www.YeOldeDragonBooks.com
www.MtZionRidgePress.com
@MichelleLevigne

Look for Michelle's Goodreads groups:
Guardians of Neighborlee
Voyages of the AFV Defender
Neighborlee Streets

NEWSLETTER:
Want to learn about upcoming books, book launch parties, inside information, and cover reveals?
Go to Michelle's website or blog to sign up.

Also by Michelle L. Levigne

Guardians of the Time Stream: 4-book Steampunk series
The Match Girls: Humorous inspirational romance series starting
    with **A Match (Not) Made in Heaven**
Sarai's Journey: A 2-book biblical fiction series
Tabor Heights: 20-book inspirational small town romance series.
Quarry Hall: 11-book women's fiction/suspense series
For Sale: Wedding Dress. Never Used: inspirational romance
Crooked Creek: Fun Fables About Critters and Kids: Children's
    short stories.
Do Yourself a Favor: Tips and Quips on the Writing Life. A book
    of writing advice.
To Eternity (and beyond): *Writing Spec Fic Good for Your Soul.* A
    book defending speculative fiction.
Killing His Alter-Ego: contemporary romance/suspense, taking
    place in fandom.
The Commonwealth Universe: SF series, 25 books and growing
The Hunt: 5-book YA fantasy series
Faxinor: Fantasy series, 4 books and growing
Wildvine: Fantasy series, 14 books when all released
Neighborlee: Humorous fantasy series
Zygradon: 5-book Arthurian fantasy series
AFV Defender: SF adventure series
Young Defenders: Middle Grade SF series, spin-off of *AFV Defender*
Magic to Spare: Fantasy series
Book & Mug Mysteries: cozy mystery series starting in 2022
Quest for the Crescent Moon: fantasy series starting in 2022